PENGUIN BOOKS

TURNING BACK THE SUN

Colin Thubron was born in London in 1939, a descendant of John Dryden. He left publishing to travel – mainly in Asia and North Africa, where he made documentary films that were shown on BBC and world television.

Afterwards he returned to the Middle East and wrote five books on the area, including *The Hills of Adonis* and *Journey into Cyprus*, for which he was elected a Fellow of the Royal Society of Literature. His other travel books include *Among the Russians* and *Behind the Wall*, which won the Hawthornden Prize and the Thomas Cook Travel Book Award for 1988. In 1984 the Book Marketing Council nominated him one of the twenty best contemporary writers on travel.

Colin Thubron has written three other highly praised novels, *A Cruel Madness*, which won the 1985 Silver Pen Award, *Falling*, which was shortlisted for the 1989 Sunday Express Book of the Year Award, and *Emperor*. Many of his books are published by Penguin.

COLIN THUBRON

TURNING BACK THE SUN

PENGUIN BOOKS

PENGUIN BOOKS

Published by the Penguin Group
Penguin Books Ltd, 27 Wrights Lane, London W8 5TZ, England
Penguin Books USA Inc., 375 Hudson Street, New York, New York 10014, USA
Penguin Books Australia Ltd, Ringwood, Victoria, Australia
Penguin Books Canada Ltd, 10 Alcorn Avenue, Toronto, Ontario, Canada M4V 3B2
Penguin Books (NZ) Ltd, 182–190 Wairau Road, Auckland 10, New Zealand

Penguin Books Ltd, Registered Offices: Harmondsworth, Middlesex, England

First published in Great Britain by William Heinemann Ltd 1991
Published in Penguin Books 1992
10 9 8 7 6 5 4 3 2 1

1

You can never go back. Deep ranges of mountain isolate the
town from the sea, and lift across half the skyline. From
any rooftop you may see them rising, at once threatening
and unreal. No road penetrates them, and the narrow-
gauge railway is unsure and precipitous. But the people in
this frontier-town have become inured to where they are
now. It consumes all their ambitions. Even its ugliness, they
say, is compelling. Besides, they have no residence permit
for anywhere but here.

In the town you often forget that other places exist. At
night, especially, it glitters self-contained in the circle of its
lights. On its perimeter the roads merge into scrubland so
abruptly that you pass horses standing asleep on the tarmac,
and under the last street-lamps graze desert antelopes. Then
the northern mountains are obscured in dark, and on the
other side the wilderness spreads in a huge, lightless
vacancy, and seems obscurely to breathe. All the absorbed
vapours of the day are released back into the dark, so you
imagine you can hear the whole desert sighing in a long,
unbroken exhalation.

By daylight, Rayner noticed, the town seemed self-
sufficient. It was robust, dangerous even, steeped in an
unholy vitality. Under the angry sun, its streets churned
with traffic and the pavements brimmed with an appearance of business: men and women in styleless shirts and
trousers, forcing transactions, chasing appointments, selling
things. Its municipal buildings, conceived in a squat style of
Doric Greek — the Court House, the Municipality, the

Department of Transport and Works — might have been raised for a miniature nation. But around them the shops and offices elbowed one another in an earthbound sprawl. They were built of concrete, or of the blood-coloured local stone, and above their awnings the shopping-malls belched up a mélange of thickset façades. There was nothing older than a century.

When Rayner first arrived from the capital fifteen years ago, sick with insomnia after two nights on the railway, he had passed under a makeshift arch of welcome blazoned 'We've got everything here'. During the next few years he had heard the same expression often, spoken in the town's clipped patter, but edged with an odd disillusion. Yet he had believed it then (he was only nineteen).

Even at that time it was called a 'purpose town'. Nobody arrived for pleasure. They came — or were sent — to engage in industry or administration. The town became their pleasure incidentally. They made money. Their residence permit, the tyrannical blue booklet of government control, shackled them to the place for life, and to them the distant capital became more like a memory-trace than a real city. Even Rayner, who was angry and nostalgic, sometimes imagined that he had never been anywhere but here.

Yet there were days when he saw a different town. Avoiding the streets' crush at noon, he would sometimes go into one of the big, heavy-carpeted bars where people sat in near-silence over their lagers or aquavit. Then he would sense the town's desperation. He saw it in the people's faces when they were alone. They looked haunted. They belonged to no real community. They were a conflation of exiles. You only had to read the owners' names above the shops: Pacini, Ridderbusch, Smith, Seifert, Ling, Moreau . . . A superficial sameness of dress or manner might unite them, but if you looked or listened closer the town lost all identity. A murmur of unfamiliar accents and dialects undermined it: men and women with the faint idioms, the

2

gestures and physiognomy, the memories, of somewhere else. In the privacy of their homes they clung to the flotsam of a lost security. The immigrant Lebanese and Syrians returned at night to neat bungalows, like other people, but once inside they sipped their coffee around trays of Damascus brass and sat on inlaid *kursi*. The Cantonese hung their walls with reproduction scrolls, and on their Western tables sat little trays of Taoist water-gardens. Latvians sang cold Nordic songs in the streets. A *barrio* of Filipinos imported their own mongo beans and noodles, and in the German Club the bar was carved with the heraldic arms of Hohenstaufen counts. Czechs, Poles, Greeks, Italians, Hungarians – they heard of their motherlands' betterment or sufferings only with a dimmed guilt or dissociation. They belonged here now, or nowhere.

As for the capital – the shimmering city on the coast which had first harboured them and where many had been born – they seemed purposely to exclude all mention of it from their talk.

Once it had accommodated everything meaningful in the colony: wealth, administration, political faith. But by the end of the nineteenth century the city had overflowed, and the drift of people south into the savage hinterland had begun. During the Great War the dictatorship had regulated all movement, resettling populations by financial inducement or brute force, and even now, far into the thirties, the economic pressures which push people to the frontier-towns are hardened by government decree. Often the whole country seems immobilised, locked into self-contained provinces, like a house without passageways.

Rayner's medical partner, an elderly Pole, told him bitterly, 'You overestimate the people in this town. They may look preoccupied, but they're not *thinking* anything. They can't afford to. They're like animals. Sophisticated animals. They live day to day.' So perhaps they were not melancholy after all, Rayner thought, just inert. Above their beer mugs

3

and whisky glasses their eyes seemed blank and undreaming. Then he thought, I've just read into them my own state.

He was less assimilated than anybody here. He had been assigned to the town's medical school from the capital, then posted to a local practice; and nothing could bring about a reversal. The town needed doctors. In the capital his parents were both dead, and he could summon no compassionate grounds for his return there except: *over there is my home.* Which was not enough.

The children of his patients, watching him, would giggle uncomfortably and whisper, 'Doctor Eagle!' (after a character in their comic books). He was a little awesome. You would not have thought that a man of thirty-four had had time to look like that – charged with such contradictory expression. The whole man gave out an exacting mixture of fierceness and sympathy. And he still looked young. But he walked with an angry, flamboyant limp from a leg shattered in a car crash. His right shoulder jerked upward as his right foot cleared the ground. To others he sometimes seemed to brandish this limp like a congenital injustice; but in fact he had almost forgotten it. Only occasionally he wondered if some bitterness had not seeped up from his foot into his brain.

But he liked to walk. He did most of his rounds on foot. In different humours he found different towns here: a place of crude vigour, a town of blinkered pragmatism, a city of pure loss. It was its isolation, he supposed, which made it seem so important. The wilderness pressed on it like a corset, crushing its energies inward. If it had any unifying trait, it was that of an insidious unease, like a distant apprehension of peril. Extrovert but self-protective, it had turned its back on the wilderness around it and looked inward, instead, on its own broad streets and squares, its fever of getting and spending, on its own miraculous presence in the emptiness.

4

But of couse you couldn't exclude that wilderness. The vista at the end of most streets was closed by a low, unbreaking wave of violet hills. Blood-coloured crags and ridges surged along the northern suburbs and burst up even in the town's heart. On the outskirts, two-lane roads stopped dead, petering into tracks or stones. Between habitation and desert was only a step. All around the town's north and west a maze of butchered hills marked the site of earlier mines and kilns, where the earth had turned sulphurous and shone with a matt glare. Their slopes rose in tiers of russet and white, twisted with dead trees where the rains had sieved down a scree powdered to dust.

But it was on the far side of the town that the real wilderness began. The houses turned their backs on it. It spread in a huge emptiness of plains, glazed only by saltbush and eucalyptus trees, and by the tarns where the natives watered their cattle. Everything out of its earth grew up bleached and ghostly; washed-out greys and silvers. Here and there a track moved into nowhere. It was a mysterious, uninscribed land, ancient and empty. It fascinated Rayner. On a clear morning, across the farthest savannah, he could make out knolls and dried rivers moving away to a level, violet horizon – the depthless violet of all this antique country, which seemed to promise nothing beyond itself.

Even the town's river followed laws of its own. It was heavy and fast and malt-coloured. Some boardwalks and jetties covered its fringe of green, and there were boats on it: a police launch and some pleasure dinghies with names like *Sunburst* and *Elsinore*. Yet the river went nowhere. It simply died in the wilderness three hundred kilometres to the south.

At first the owner of the *Seagull* ignored the faint, regular thudding under his bows. It sounded like a rotted treetrunk: something soft and stiff. Then he went and peered over the side, and let out a breathy, high-pitched, '*God!*'

Later Rayner recognised the day as a turning-point,

5

announced by the frightened tap of the messenger's fingers on his clinic door. A big crowd had gathered on the river bank. Two policemen had pulled the bodies into the shallows but now stood uncertain, as if afraid to lift them into the daylight. They deferred to him with relief. It seemed callous, for some reason, to remove his shoes and socks before entering the water, so he waded straight in to where the two corpses floated in one another's arms. They drifted on their sides, swollen and blackened. The crowd hovered motionless. His hands started trembling. The corpses knocked against his shins. They were bound face to face, like lovers, and their heads had been axed in from behind. He circled one in his arms and closed his eyes, then pulled towards the bank. They came together.

On shore, the disintegrating hand of one corpse slipped its bonds, leaving part of itself behind like a glove, and released the bodies to lie side by side. Rayner had seen many dead, but none like these. Their bloated trunks had burst their clothes – the man's trousers tangled round his ankles, the woman's dress split top to bottom – and their faces were ebony balloons. He knelt by them helplessly, his revulsion stronger than his pity. Their eyes had sunk to milky slits. Their dilated tongues stuck out through their lips.

He did not know what to do. 'Has anyone called an ambulance?'

He wiped the froth from their noses and mouths. Inspecting closer, he wondered if he might recognise one of them. But they were beyond recognition. Out of their blackened skulls the hair flowed white and gold. It was the only natural thing left to them, yet it seemed more violent and artificial than the rest. It was the woman's hair which filled him with new horror. He was sure he recognised it, its distinctive champagne colour, even the way its damp folds settled round her head. But when he looked at what had

6

once been her, nothing came to mind. Only long after did he realise of whom the hair had reminded him.

In the back of each head the axe-blow had left a jagged trench. It was the traditional way by which the natives killed, and now a man edged forward from the crowd, stared into the dead faces and said, 'That's what the savages do! They hit you like that!'

The crowd loosened, then surged to look closer. A fat woman suddenly cried out, 'God help me, I know them! It's the Mordaunts from the farm up the railtrack!' She plucked her husband's arm. 'It's the Mordaunts, Gyorgy. That's her dress.'

The man stared stonily. 'They're burnt.' He demanded, 'Why are they burnt like that? They've turned them black!'

Two small boys, jubilant and trembling, piped, 'They've turned them black!'

People's voices spurted and whispered. Someone said, 'Corpses always go black.' But it was as if a blast of wind had hit them.

Rayner's voice sounded too loud, and for some reason angry. 'That's blood pigment in the skin.' He felt he was quelling something monstrous. 'That's quite normal. The blood dries.'

But he knew how strange it seemed. The woman had floated uppermost, on her front, so that gravity had drawn the pigment dark over her breast and face and she gleamed like bronze. Whereas the man had lain face upwards, and the discoloration had spread only to his back, leaving his chest white and his face a soapy blur of decay.

One of the policemen said, 'That's the Mordaunts' farm was ransacked a week ago. We couldn't find them. How long you reckon they've been in the water?'

Rayner said, 'About a week.' They'd probably been killed a few hours before immersion, he thought; blackening and saponification were both far gone.

By the time an ambulance came, the crowd had swelled

to hundreds. They stood tense and quiet as the bodies were taken away. Rayner did not know if the coldness opening in his stomach meant fear of the natives or something else. As the people began dispersing they became suddenly agitated, like bacilli hurrying the news down all the town's arteries.

2

The natives called themselves *naugalad*, or 'savage ones', and they carried this forbidding name with the pride of a people still steeped in fierce separateness. To be 'savage' was to be uncontaminated, free. So they turned the word from an insult into a dignity.

Yet it was strange how in town you scarcely noticed them. They filtered in to buy tools and trinkets sometimes, dressed in threadbare trousers and dresses, with old straw hats or kepis on their heads, then sat motionless for hours on the steps and benches of the shopping-mall. They had thick, trunk-like bodies and delicate feet and hands. Hour after hour, utterly still, they would glare ahead of them with a furious, impenetrable fixity, as if straining at something which obscured the present from them. Occasionally, in the busier streets, you might glimpse the women wandering bewildered with distended stomachs and undersized babies.

On the early maps of this region the whole void south and east of the town was spanned by the one word: 'uninhabited'. And people still behaved as if the savages did not exist. Most of them looked inexplicably old, like emanations of this land which the white men could not trust. With their gnarled foreheads and scrawny limbs, they reminded Rayner of stricken trees. Occasionally on the mall they would get up and shout incomprehensibly to one another before walking away with a light, noiseless gait on the balls of their feet. But generally they moved among the rosy-skinned townsmen like shadows. They might have been invisible.

Those who stayed in town were very few: a handful of domestics and low-paid miners. The whites called them 'tame' ones. A few more would camp temporarily in the dried river beds along the outskirts. From his bungalow overlooking the river, Rayner would see them squatted on their blankets, declaiming poetry, it seemed, or sagas. Usually one of them would be posturing in a circle of others: mahogany-faced women and lax, half-naked men, whose backs and shoulders were matted with wiry hair. At night their fires flickered for hours and he could hear – uncomprehending – every sing-song syllable. But by morning they would be gone.

They fascinated and vaguely disturbed him. They could exist on almost nothing, he'd heard, living off sandalwood berries or gathering seeds and roots; and in regions where any other people would have died, they sucked the moisture from obscure tubers and ate insects. Some symbiotic veneration for the earth increased their latent horror of the white men. The whites, they said, had hurt the earth unforgivably, carving and quartering it into roads and mines. Yet the savages, he knew, killed without conscience, as a kind of jocular sport, as if people were of no importance. Rocks and trees were more permanent. They worshipped rocks and trees.

Rayner's villa was more like their nomad's camps than he recognised. For seven years he had inhabited it as if he would move out next week, and its most personal ornaments were fragments of petrified wood and coloured pebbles which he'd gathered from the wilderness. He still felt as if the place were not his. That was the only way he could endure it, he thought, or endure the town, or perhaps anything. A state of transition. It was spacious and silent, lit by long windows with long green blinds. All its colours were cool. Its ceilings sighed with wood-bladed fans. Nearly all signs of personal life – photographs, papers, mementoes – were out of sight in the louvred cupboards. If Rayner could have expressed himself in décor, this rented space, with its inherited pallor and coolness, might be what he would have chosen.

All the same, it enclosed his rage. From his windows he could see half the town: its gridiron order, its smokestacks. He felt a duty to it, sometimes even a tenderness, but it filled him with unbearable claustrophobia. It seemed thin, narrow, almost without quality. And he felt himself growing thin and narrow with it. The town was superficially pleased by itself. He hated that. Its skyline was just itself. Sometimes, remembering the capital, he wanted to shout in the streets, 'Is this *all*?'

He had started to drink a bit, whisky mostly. Returning late from his evening rounds he'd thought, I must watch this. But his one glass had become two, then three. His mother had drunk too. But there was too much of his father in him, he thought, to let it go that far; and one day, as if in his father's honour, he simply stopped.

But the episode left him uneasy. He could no longer quite predict himself. Soon afterwards, coming upon some photographic portraits in his desk, he found himself hunting them for an explanation. But his parents stared back at him out of another age. The cut of his father's hair and lawyer's dress looked austerely archaic; and his mother's face was cradled in the side-curls fashionable twenty years ago. And her dress – did they still dress like that in the capital?

Yet he thought of his parents' traits as alternating in him. Even their faces. He recognised his father's features in his own harsh cheeks and hectoring eyes. They shared the same angry, overhung brows. But when he looked in the mirror he saw, between his father's nose and firm chin, his mother's mouth smiling. And in calmer moods, as if it superposed itself at moments of his father's inattention, he would sense the whole stamp of his expression overcast by hers.

There were times when he could not disentangle in

11

himself his father's solitude and ferocious spirit of enquiry from his mother's sentimental longings and compassion. Often now he was flooded by an incontinent sympathy for people as he talked with them – for a patient, a girlfriend, or just an acquaintance – and after they had left him he would clean forget them. He saw himself oscillating between pity and isolated indifference. He expended more energy on the town than almost anyone he knew: he had even started an advisory service to the more distant cattle stations, and his voice over the shaky radiotelegraph must have saved women in childbirth from fatal septicaemia. Yet for all his apparent commitment, his energy, a profound inner betrayal separated him off.

He wanted to return to the capital.

Nowadays the car crash which had killed his mother and maimed his own foot, together with his exile from the capital – all within three months – struck him as a severance from any understanding of himself. He had never afterwards seen himself a continuous person. His first nineteen years seemed to have been lived dreaming. Sometimes he fancied that his parents had died with the secret of him, and that if only he could return to the capital he might recover it.

3

'People say the savages have this idol out in the desert, where there's a freshwater spring. They pretend it talks to them.'

Rayner said, 'We pretend God talks to us.'

'I think you do.' Ivar looked at him in a way which merged scorn with affection so indissolubly that Rayner could not be annoyed. He remembered this derisive fondness from their schooldays in the capital: Ivar, stocky in his green neckscarf and jumper, saying, 'Come on, Rayner. Are you one of my gang or not?'

They sat in a cave of dimmed light and music. It was rather a ritzy nightclub for a town like this, Rayner thought. It sported a cabaret with striptease, and four or five hostesses of various appeal. The waitresses, including a sad, sexless transvestite, glided between the tables in high-collared jackets and fishnet tights. Rayner wondered who came here. They seemed mostly to be young businessmen and a few army officers like Ivar.

Rayner said vaguely, 'I've usually met women without all this paraphernalia.' The place reeked of something new to him (but anything new in this town was a relief): an ambience of the sin-market, of sexual peril. It was fleetingly provocative.

Ivar said, 'They're a decent lot of girls here. And you don't *pay* them, remember, you *give them presents*.'

Rayner laughed uneasily. 'You do, I go home.'

From time to time Ivar and he indulged the uncritical friendship of old schoolmates. Yet they also held off from

13

one another. They were too deeply unlike. Ivar's features smoothed into one another like cement. He seemed to spread calm about him. His low-lidded eyes held an intelligence unconfused by passion or (Rayner suspected) much conscience. It was the face of a man inspecting an orderly room; whereas Rayner's glared into chaos. Rayner seemed to conduct a running quarrel with the world in which Ivar was at home. They slightly tantalised one another.

But Ivar was also a source of information. He was second-in-command of the garrison here: a callow-looking company of the Fourth Field Army in what the military still called a 'key frontier-town'. And Rayner could not resist leaning forward under the din of the music and saying, 'Did they find out anything about the murders?'

Ivar said, 'That was a police job.'

'But you've increased your patrols, haven't you? Or is all that driving about in jeeps just to reassure us?'

Ivar looked at him in a way which Rayner remembered, with the watching smile of someone who uses intimacies like a weapon. Even in their schooldays, Ivar has been the wielder of secret knowledge. Now he said, 'There's been another killing. Just this morning. An old man in one of those smallholdings. Had a spear in the side. They just took his cattle-food and wireless. And that was just four kilometres from here.'

Rayner said, 'It must be the failed rains. Perhaps they're getting desperate.'

Ivar shook his head. 'I think they enjoy killing. They kill for almost nothing.' He said in the same level, comfortable tone, 'If we adopted their code, they'd be rounded up tomorrow and eliminated.'

'You talk as if you want to.'

'It would be more rational.' Ivar spoke with neither rancour nor regret. 'Because they can't adapt. If a species fails to adapt, it dies.'

Rayner thought: no, they can't adapt. That is what's

14

fascinating about them. He remembered their night fires along the river, the unintelligible words of their chanting. 'I don't know anything about them,' he said.

'The evidence is that war is a religion with them. Their idol is a kind of war-god.'

'How did you hear that?'

'The older settlers had it from missionaries. That's why the missionaries never made any headway, they say. The savages had their own god already. They never understood Christianity. They got confused by the Trinity.'

Rayner said harshly, 'So do I.'

Ivar smiled into his brandy. The music almost dinned out the words. 'You always were a pighead. I remember that.'

'Do you?' Rayner did not remember it.

'You always got in a hell of a passion about things, then walked away into your own world and forgot. Do you remember the time we planned . . .'

Occasionally, as now, something Ivar said shocked Rayner into memory, and he'd think: so I can't have changed much after all. He asked caustically, 'Where's this idol meant to be, then? Out in the middle of nowhere?'

'Not exactly.' Ivar became suddenly discreet. Rayner had the impression that he'd put on his uniform. 'It's on our maps.'

Even as a boy, Ivar had been impressive, Rayner remembered. He'd been expert at the disclosure or withholding of information. Information, even then, was power. He'd always known which teachers to manipulate, how to get cheap cigarettes, the best crib-sheets.

'So you're preparing to round them up.'

'You can't usually find them. If you hunt them, they just dissolve . . .'

But a pair of woman's arms had arrived round Ivar's neck. She was tall, with cornflower eyes and a small head misted in maize-coloured hair. She was the reason Ivar had come. Her eyes wandered over Rayner. 'I'm Felicie,' she

15

said. 'My father owns this place.' He felt her assessing him: money, age, sexuality ... but she did so with a distrait candour, and he realised he was smiling at her. 'This is Zoë.' she said. 'I sing. She's a dancer.'

She settled by Ivar as of right, while Zoë – a silent, fiercely made-up girl – sat by Rayner but looked in the other direction. They were not the prostitutes Rayner had expected. He was unsure what they were. They were not even typical artistes. Felicie talked in a rapid, lost voice with her arms circled round Ivar. Was it true what she'd heard about the savages, she asked? Might they attack the town? Perhaps by night . . .

Ivar drank his brandy between her locked arms. Nothing was true, he said.

She released him petulantly. 'God, I hate this town. And now we're going to be murdered in it.'

'You can be murdered anywhere.'

'But it gets more violent every year. And it's so *boring*. Give me the capital any day. God, I *love* the capital!' But she spoke as if it didn't matter. Hating this or loving that was a pastime. She looked vaguely, perpetually out of focus, Rayner thought. She reached over and shook Zoë's arm. 'Did you see the latest? Scoop-back gowns are back in fashion. In the capital . . .'

But Zoë did not answer, and Felicie focused suddenly on Rayner. 'I haven't seen you around before. Are you from the capital?'

'Years ago,' Rayner said. He suppressed the ruefulness in his voice. 'Fifteen years.' But he did not want to discuss it with her.

Felicie murmured, 'Fifteen years.' She stroked Ivar's cheek, while he kissed her lips, so that Rayner turned to Zoë and asked woodenly, 'What kind of dancing do you do?'

She looked at him for the first time. Compared with Felicie, she seemed perfectly, violently concentrated: a too-immaculate face, browned and powdered and lit by glittering pale-blue eyes, which repelled enquiry. Her hair was seized back like a ballerina's and knotted in a shining scallop behind. 'The dancing's a mixture,' she said. 'Jazz, flamenco, ballet . . .'

He noticed how her fingers wrenched at one another. He had thought her bored or preoccupied, but instead she was nervous. She added with a trace of defiance, 'I compose my own dances.'

Rayner guessed her dances would be conventional, whereas Felicie, who under her manicured pallor seemed to be screaming, would sing in a way he could not predict.

She stood up shakily and took Zoë's hand. 'We're performing in a minute,' she said. Odd, Rayner thought, how Felicie seemed to exist underwater, her hair adrift and her movements all strengthless. She kissed Ivar's neck and smiled at Rayner. She had the kind of loose, mobile mouth which he found attractive.

The curtains parted before a small stage with a backdrop of mirrors and hanging strips of silver. The tables were starting to fill up with youths who had come in from late-night bars or from one of the licensed brothels. Shouts of, 'Where's the strippers?' went up, and, 'Get on with it!'

But the revue had been programmed to titillate. The first to take the stage was a middle-aged acrobat who suspended himself lugubriously between aluminium poles. Then came a skinny contortionist, who twined around herself so effortlessly that Rayner stopped being surprised at anything she did. Yet this furtive venue – the plush, converted cellar with its blue spotlights and recorded cymbals and drums – lent to these acts a hint of the forbidden. If they'd been performed in one of the town squares, he thought, they would have gone almost ignored. But here, in the theatre of secrecy, in the dramatised dark, people paid to watch, and were waiting. Their heads clustered black along the tables

17

nearest the stage. Their camaraderie had dwindled to crude expectation.

Ivar's eyes flickered between bar and stage and floor. He was totting up costs and income, and eventually said, 'Felicie's father must make a packet out of this rubbish.'

'Is she your girlfriend now?' Rayner had watched Ivar change girlfriends unscathed. Of all the enigmas in Ivar, this was the deepest and most enviable to him.

'Yes. But I'm not interested in her money. She's just a nice girl. A bit simple. Her people came from the capital twenty years ago, and she's got this fantasy about going back.'

'I don't blame her,' Rayner said. 'What's there for her here?' He noticed Ivar flinch with annoyance. 'Unless you're serious about her.'

Ivar said, 'There's no point in her dreaming of going back when she can't. This town is basically as good as anywhere else.' He spoke in the reasonable tones which at once impressed and maddened Rayner – Ivar so reeked of comfort and self-control. 'There's nothing in the capital that you can't buy here. I've been away twelve years now and I don't miss a thing. Not a thing.'

Rayner was amazed. 'Christ, Ivar, don't you remember *anything*? Do you *really* not remember? You may be able to buy the same things – I can't recall much of that – but the whole spirit of the capital is different. It's another climate, different history, different – You must remember the *girls*, at least. Just take our gang. Jarmila, Miriam, Adelina . . .'

'There are plenty of girls here.'

'But they don't think the same way.' Rayner heard his own cruelty, he couldn't help it. 'They've no – no quality. And how could they have? Things are tough here. It's not only the way people look. This is a practical place. Possessions, entertainment. There's nothing more. Does anybody talk about anything else here?' His words grew loud against the music. 'God, Ivar you *must* remember. The capital just breeds another kind of person. Perhaps it's because the sea's there, while we've only got desert . . .'

But a slow frown had gathered on Ivar's forehead. He just said, 'I think it's much the same everywhere. And even if it isn't, you have to adjust.' He touched Rayner's arm with the strange, sudden warmth which always surprised Rayner: a concession to their schooldays, to the shared past, a leftover (Rayner felt, ironically) from the lost capital. 'If you don't adjust, you're history.'

Rayner thought: he must be protecting himself, he must remember as well as I do.

Rayner remembered them in the capital walking through a park by the ever-present sea. Over the years this image had often recurred to him, yet it recorded a moment of so little import that he wondered why it was by this that he so often remembered the city. Perhaps the picture had implanted itself simply because it was typical. But there they were, Ivar and he, with Miriam and Jarmila between them, wandering through the autumn leaves of giant syca-mores, while beside them ran the wrought-iron railings ubiquitous in the city: heavy, grand and thickened by a hundred repaintings; and beyond them rose their own tall, terraced houses. In this image all their surroundings were much older than they were, and he thought of this ancient-ness – a benign security stretching back almost for ever – as peculiar to the capital.

Suddenly the curtains parted and Felicie appeared, touch-ing a microphone to her lips like a baby's dummy. A see-through chiffon dress tinged her white body in watery blue. Her bare feet poked out waifishly beneath it, and her head was coddled in a silver cap flecked with small wings, like an effete Valkyrie.

Then she sang, and for the first and last time that evening Rayner felt like a voyeur. Every other artiste had shaped a real performance, however inept, but under Felicie's foolish costume and *ingénue* masquerade was only her naked self,

and this she gave in the pathetic confidence that it must
have value.

> *Sometimes at night I dream*
> *I'm in your arms again*
> *Sometimes at night return*
> *To that lost room*

Rayner felt he was staring into a vacuum: just borrowed
yearnings and self-pity. Her voice whimpered and squeaked
like a mouse. If the proprietor had not been her father, he
thought, she wouldn't have passed an audition. He found
himself deeply, inexplicably pained by it, as if he were
somehow himself the victim of her humiliation. And he
dared not even look at Ivar.

> *If you remember me*
> *I'll journey home . . .*

Yet when the curtains closed on her, there was desultory
clapping. The bleary music continued. The audience went
on knocking back its eau-de-vie. Nobody seemed to have
noticed anything, or to have shared his vicarious pain. Ivar
just smiled at him suavely and said, 'You won't find many
women of thirty looking like that.'

So Ivar had not listened to her, Rayner thought – and
who could blame him? He'd just watched her body. 'Yes,'
Rayner said, 'she's . . . pretty' – and the word extinguished
her.

'You could make a decent life here with the right girl,'
Ivar said. 'Men of our age should think of settling down.
Not much more of this . . .' He gestured at the stage, where
the first of the strippers was starting on her ritual of petty
disclosures and delays.

Ivar passed laconic judgement on them. 'Bottom's too
slack . . . that one won't last . . . good breasts . . . there's
ugly muscle tone . . .' – and about one, a coffee-skinned

20

siren with the betraying loose limbs and knotted brows of another people: 'Reckon she's got savage blood.'

To Rayner each turn seemed more vapid than the last. The girls entered dressed as geishas, cats, houris, schoolmistresses, chatelaines. As they peeled off their veils and wimples and smocks, he felt as clinical towards them as to the women he examined each morning for pregnancy or breast cancer. 'Do they do it for money?'

'No,' Ivar said. 'They get paid a pittance.'

So their mystery deepened.

From time to time their acts were broken by interludes of conjuring or song, and in one of these Zoë appeared. She was accompanied by violent music. In its mask of powder and eye-shadow, she had recreated her face not for human intimacy but for theatrical display. He saw this now. It projected her with schematic vividness. The stringent ballerina's hairdo withdrew all softening from her battle-plan of upcurved mouth and highlit cheekbones. She was fiercely attractive.

She released herself headlong into the music. Her dancing was as she'd said, an amalgam of her own: a tumult of twisting, leaping and mime, out of which – as if from early training – erupted balletic pirouettes and arabesques. She seemed to dance out of some defiant core in her, without thought of her audience. The music throbbed and swung. Every movement shouted: this is *me*! Even her figure, encased in a vulgar iridescent leotard, came as a surprise. Her torso with its long, delicate arms and soft-looking breasts, descended to full hips and strong dancer's legs. She seemed less sexual than violently, daemonically physical.

Rayner sensed the audience go still: confronted by the unexpected. In the screen of mirrors behind the stage they were all reflected as a diffused whiteness, like dead fish floating in the dark, while the fierce, small figure in the leotard, cut low behind down a shimmering brown back, flung herself angrily at their indifference.

21

They confused her dance with striptease. At several tables the men were growing restless. Somebody shouted up: 'Get yer clothes off!'

Rayner wondered why the club engaged her, unless as a foil to the strippers. In this underworld of spangled G-strings and rouged nipples, she emerged as an enigma, only half tamed. She'd somehow got away.

Rayner said: 'She doesn't seem to care about her audience.'

'She cares all right,' Ivar said, 'but she's self-centred.' His lips compressed sourly. Rayner thought he detected a hint of hurt pride, which in Ivar was odd. Zoë was the only performer on whose body he passed no judgement. Perhaps, Rayner thought, he was too familiar with it.

'She got left behind,' Ivar laughed, 'like the savages.'

'Left behind?'

'Yes, this place started up ten years ago as a satirical cabaret. Pretentious stuff. Can you imagine it, in this town? And of course nobody came. The government didn't even bother to close it down. It just faded out. Felicie's father bought it for a song, and the old troupe gave up. All except Zoë. She never accepts anything. The club kept her on as "something different".' He sounded slightly bitter. 'One day she'll dance herself to death.'

In the middle of Zoë's act, Felicie returned to their table. Rayner went on staring at the stage, refusing to comment on her singing, but Ivar told her, 'You're beautiful.' She smiled and followed Rayner's gaze. She said, 'I can't stand Zoë when she's like this. She's so cold.'

By now the spectators, in their lethargic way, were reacting as never before. Their dislike arose not in shouted abuse but in a diffused murmur of resentment which came welling up out of the dark. It was extraordinary. By her dance's end an almost tangible wave of anger was beating against the stage. After the strippers' open thighs, this other performance struck the half-drunk audience as an insult.

The girl was flattering herself instead of them, making shapes with her too-independent body. And her inaccessibility was unbearable.

Her only concession to eroticism happened a minute before she ended. Then she literally let down her hair. It fell brown and shining to her waist. It transformed her. It lengthened and gentled her face. And all at once she looked unsure. To Rayner it seemed as if this was her way of undressing – a way more self-exposing than any of the others'. She no longer looked like a woman, but a young girl. She finished in stillness, but the eyes staring out between the frame of hair were now tentative, and seemed suddenly to need the audience's applause, which did not come.

Even Rayner's lonely clapping sounded not for her pastiche dance, but for the courage with which she had invested it. She left him vaguely confused. He had misjudged her. After a while he got up to leave. Ivar had turned moody, Felicie was drunk, and the rest of the audience were concentrating on another stripper, as if Zoë's dance was no more than a failed version of this one. And maybe it was, Rayner thought. He was always laying his own meanings on simple things, he knew. And perhaps Zoë was as empty as Felicie in her way: just an exuberant girl, dancing.

4

'What do you mean when you say you're "cut off"?'

But Rayner did not know. Perhaps to feel cut off was to have grown up. He said, 'I don't feel I belong here.'

The man said, 'I'm not sure that anybody does. This is such a peculiar place.'

'Other people accept it,' Rayner said. He glanced at the man, wondering how recent an immigrant or exile he was. 'But I can't put down roots here. I want to, but I can't.'

'Does that hurt?'

He said, 'Enough to convince me that I have to go somewhere else – but I don't know how.' He met the analyst's gaze, but could not read it. 'I wouldn't have come to you if it weren't a professional requirement.'

If the man felt affronted, he did not show it. In this country, as elsewhere, anyone seeking psychiatric training had to submit to analysis himself. Yet the town contained only this school medical officer, whose own grounding went little deeper than a dabbling in books sent from Europe.

Perhaps it was because Rayner felt no respect for the officer – an angular, puzzled-looking man – that he expressed his alienation in irate bursts. 'I feel I'm wasting away here.' He felt this almost physically sometimes. 'I can't even do a real job . . . Sometimes I wonder if I'm treating human beings at all. Days go by without my patients asking me a single question about their condition, why they're suffering – nothing. I might as well be treating cattle. This sounds harsh, but that's how it is . . . and the hospital's hopelessly short of specialists. I've found myself doing jobs I'm virtually unqualified for. An ordinary doctor in the capital would never be sewing up some of the wounds which I've sewn. But here it's common practice.'

The man said: 'I suppose it's practical, country medicine.'

'It's terrifying.'

'But you're needed here, aren't you? Respected.'

'Am I?' Rayner laughed, but with a trace of bitterness. 'That just lowers my respect for others.'

The officer asked, 'But where do you want to go?'

Rayner answered with faint surprise, 'The capital.' Where else, he wondered, did anyone want to go? Recently he had published some articles on psoriasis, the skin disease – the hospital laboratory had rudimentary facilities for analysing it – and he still hoped for a transfer to the dermatology unit in the capital. He'd take any job they offered.

'The capital . . .' The analyst started jotting things on his pad. 'You were born in the capital?'

'Yes.' Rayner became mesmerised by the man's forehead as he wrote. Its dust of greying hair receded in uneven clumps, as if it had been swept by a bush fire. He imagined the swarm of trite thoughts that might be entering it, and said curtly, 'My childhood was happy. It was just too brief.'

'Your parents . . .'

'My father died when I was fourteen, my mother five years later. In a car crash. That's how I got this.' He flourished his twisted foot.

The analyst, he knew now, would edge him towards his childhood. Yet this did not spring up in the simple, sharp pictures which the man must want, but in composite images accrued over months and years – images which seemed to stand surety, by their very ordinariness, for a whole season, or place, or person.

In the summer of his fifteenth birthday his mother had rented a villa by the sea, but his memories of it had resolved into pictures from which everything temporary – all movement, guests, bird-flight – had been eliminated, like a camera-shot on so long an exposure that only the essential and permanent ingrained itself. He could remember the jagged circle of every rock-pool which perforated the shore at low tide, and each item of the villa's furniture. Yet in his memory the place was unpeopled. Where had his mother been? He did not know. His images of her now were pathetically selective and few. And the effort to preserve these remnants had turned them too familiar, blurred by use, not memories of a woman any more, just memories of memories.

He did not know how much of his mother he could accurately reproduce for the analyst. But the man said, 'Tell me what she was to you. Her reality to you.'

But even then she did not appear easily. He remembered her as a pervasive presence more than a physical fact. He had been a solitary child, and he perceived this mother of his boyhood not as a spectator or confidante, but as a benign voice off-stage. Of her real life at that time, he could piece together almost nothing.

'Who do you prefer,' she had once asked him, 'your father or me?' and the fact that he remembered this question, and the intensity in her soft, sallow face, was a little strange. But he was only five, and he answered, 'You.'

Later she became fixed more securely in his memory, inseparable from the big, airy house with its bleached furnishings and feel of internal sunlight. Its dreamy spaces suited her. She was absent-mindedly tender. After his father's death, the flushed cheeks and dishevelled hair of her occasional drinking touched him with alarm. Perhaps they had become too used to happiness, he thought, because he did not know this other woman.

'Until then I hadn't thought of understanding her.'

The analyst did not answer.

Rayner said irritably, 'I suppose this is somehow meant to affect my relationships with women now.'

26

The man inclined his strange head, as if listening.

Yet when Rayner thought of these relationships, they seemed too amorphous to describe. However impassioned – and some had preoccupied him for years – they had been conducted in the knowledge that one day he would leave here. His final commitment was to somewhere else. He said, 'I haven't found anyone right for me.' He sounded apologetic, even to himself. 'Perhaps I've unconsciously chosen women unsuitable to marry . . . because I know I won't stay.'

'What do you mean "unsuitable to marry"?'

Rayner was ashamed of this. But he blundered on. 'They've been much older, or had a different education – or were married already . . .' He disliked the person saying this. Even at the outset of these affairs, he'd been dogged by this betrayal, the knowledge of their transience. Yet he had gone on with them. Several of these women had come to love him, as he cooled towards them. In a town like this, they continued like ghosts: the secretary in the office window whose eyes still followed him in the street; Xenia, greying now, turning her face feverishly away from him at parties; Myra, who still sold scarves on the mall.

The man said, 'Have you ever felt committed to anyone?'

'I fell in love in the capital. But I was only nineteen.'

He had known her since childhood. She was one of the small band with whom he'd grown up: children marked out by a modest privilege of which they were scarcely aware. The letters from these friends had petered out years ago, but he sometimes wondered what had become of them: the gifted and melancholy Leon, who must surely be an artist or writer by now (although he'd heard nothing of him); and Gerhard, pushy and handsome, a friend of Ivar's. The girls were such close friends that they seemed to partake a little of one another's aura, of the same optimism and clarity. At least in retrospect, they were beautiful, with their blue and hazel eyes and blonde or fair-streaked hair. They

27

emanated laughter and trust, and a little vanity. Even Adelina, whose features were so irregular, partook of this mutual glamour with her long, slender legs and innocent haughtiness.

But Miriam's attraction was different. She had dark hair and dark eyes. Even as a boy he'd known why the other girls appealed to him; but with Miriam he was unsure. While the others were expressed by their faces — pretty, even beautiful faces — Miriam's personality stirred in her whole body, which was vigorous and full.

In the brief months between his car crash and his transfer from the capital, he had fallen in love with her. Later he wondered if this love had been ignited by her radiant health, viewed from his sickbed through weakened eyes. But they never slept together. The capital was a puritan city. They lived under public scrutiny, in clubs and restaurants. In the gang of their friends, they did not noticeably pair off. The group held its members in common. Now he could not even be sure how exclusive he had been to her, but remembered their lovemaking as a glory of nervous, adolescent exploration in the evening parks during autumn.

They used to go diving together on the coral west of the capital. After his discharge from hospital he forced himself to do this again, but one morning he found to his horror that he could not squeeze his damaged foot into its flipper. For several minutes he stood up in the boat, furious with humiliation, while the others went overboard; and when at last he dropped into the water and descended the anchor-chain behind Miriam, the divemaster never noticed that he was barefoot.

Rayner did not know it then, but this would be the last time he would see her. He felt a little sick. The rasp of a strong current clouded the water with a dust of coral fragments. Miriam swam ahead of him with languid undulations of her flippered feet. The compressed-air cylinders obscured her back. All familiarity seemed gone from her, because she had dyed her dark hair pale – a smoky gold colour, which flowed out behind her. Even when she turned, her face floated enigmatic behind its mask and regulator, washed by this flaxen strangeness.

He came alongside her with strenuous thrusts of his unaided feet. The others were ahead, oblivious of them. The current had eased now, and the water cleared. In a dreamy unison they glided together abreast, as if flying, while the coral steepened into miniature crags around them.

Then came the moment by which he remembered their love. He reached out and took her hand. Behind its mask her face looked startled for a moment, then she pulled his hand towards her and held it clenched against her breast. The next instant, teasingly, she had taken the regulator out of her mouth and was holding it towards him. So he removed his own and gave it to her, and childishly, a little dangerously, breathing from each other's cylinders, they swam on for a full two minutes, locked side by side. It was a moment of perfect trust. They went in slow motion, weightless. They might have been breathing through each other's lungs. She still clasped his hand. They must have looked like one creature, he later thought – but an inept mutant, doomed to perish. Yet it was an instant of such eerie, unaccountable union that he imagined it afterwards more complete than the sexual coupling they had never known, and as if to illumine the moment's strangeness, great drifts of damsel-fish, confined in the coral valley, came flickering and brushing against them like cold gems.

'When did you leave?' The analyst's pen shifted over his notepad.

'Just three days later. I'd been assigned here after my exam results.' He laughed a little bitterly. 'The results weren't good. The car crash interfered with my studies.'

His friends had gathered on the station platform to say farewell and fill his arms with small gifts. But the conventional words of parting – 'Until next year!' or 'Come back and see us!' – never reached their lips. There was no such hope of return. So they spoke about small, immediate things: the appearance of his fellow-passengers, the sudden rain. Nobody could face *for ever*. Their ebullience had shrunk to helplessness. Jarmila and Adelina cried a little, and Leon was biting his lip.

Only Miriam was not there. Again and again he scrutinised the platform for her. The doors were clunking shut all along the train. The men clasped his hands. Then, at last, he realised that she would not come, and understood. Among this crowd of friends, the gap that she created – her inability to endure this last farewell – was more eloquent than any words she might have spoken. None of the others mentioned her. It was as if they conspired in the knowledge that her presence would be unbearable.

For months afterwards he imagined her face as an oval gap in that platform crowd. He could not bear to write, and nor did she. After a year she had retreated to a cell somewhere in the back of his memory, and he slipped into the arms of the girl who sold cheap scarves on the town's mall.

5

The partition wall in Rayner's clinic gave out a relentless thudding, as if someone were beating it with his fist. From the far side he heard the voice of his colleague Leszek, raised in anxiety. But the thudding went on like a threatened heartbeat, and beneath it the voice of a man: 'I want to know. I have the right to know.'

Rayner tried to concentrate on his own patient, a four-month-old baby who had spewed up all night, his mother said. The woman's voice was gravelly, suspicious. The baby had not been registered. The thudding next door continued, but the talking had died. His examination cleared the baby, but disclosed quinsy in the mother. The thudding rose to a crescendo. There was a noise of splintered glass.

When he flung open his door onto the reception area he saw the usual listless quadrangle of patients, sitting on quilts against the walls, waiting. But in his partner's room a coarse, heavy-built man hovered tempestuously above the examination couch, where a broken glass had fallen or been dashed from somebody's hand. His fist still belaboured the wall, but it was impossible to tell if he were threatening or protecting the woman who lay there. She stared at the ceiling with a face of abject tiredness.

Leszek looked at Rayner with open relief, and turned to the man. 'This is my partner. He will give you a second opinion.' His voice trembled. 'Really, I can't say anything more, because I simply don't know. We will have to carry out tests.'

'Tests?' The man looked as if he were being cheated.

'What in hell can they tell you that you don't know already?'

Leszek took off his glasses as if he no longer wanted to see. He touched Rayner's shoulder. 'The patient complains of intermittent fever and lassitude. I've carried out my examination, and taken a blood sample. There's nothing obviously wrong. The patient has a skin discoloration, which is causing her husband concern. She's noticed it for six weeks . . .'

Rayner leant over to examine her. The husband's stare dug into the back of his neck. She was one of those townswomen whose faces had outrun their bodies, leaving her features lined and sallow above a still young figure. Her arms were crossed over her breasts in embarrassment. She whispered, 'It's disgusting.'

Rayner eased her hands to her side, then stifled his surprise. Between her breasts and out from her armpits spread a dark pigmentation which he'd never seen before. It looked like liquid chocolate. Its edges ended abruptly, leaving nothing between itself and the whiteness of the normal skin.

He did not know what to say. It did not look like a fungal disease, but he asked, 'Have you felt any irritation?' The woman was silent. 'Does it itch?'

The husband said, 'Of course it itches.'

'Let her answer.' Rayner excluded him with his back.

But the woman only echoed wanly, 'Of course it itches.'

No wonder, Rayner thought. Either she or her husband had lacerated its whole surface, as if with sandpaper. 'You should have left this alone.'

'How could I?' The husband barged in beside him. 'Look at it. *Look at it*!'

Rayner was growing angry. 'Did you think it would *come off*, or what? Now will you let me complete my examination?'

But there was nothing left to examine. Leszek had

32

smeared the rash with gentian violet, but Rayner felt sure now that it was not fungal. He did not know what it was. He imagined it must spring from some hormonal imbalance, or be the benign result of nerve-cell tumours. But it did not resemble anything in his experience.

The man said, 'Well?'

'I've got nothing to add,' Rayner said. 'We'll await tests.' The woman sat up shakily, pulling on her dress. 'Once we've established the cause, your skin will return to normal with treatment.'

'Who the fuck are you telling?' The man's fists were flailing at his sides. 'That disease isn't curable, is it? Are you saying you can change it back to white? You come clean with me, doctor, that's the savage disease, isn't it?' He rammed his kepi back on his head and glared at the woman. 'That's one fucking low disease.'

Rayner turned on him. 'Who says it's a savage's disease? Where did you hear that?'

The man said, 'It's around town. It's spreading.'

What was spreading, Rayner wondered, the disease or the fallacy of its origin? He said, 'This is the first case I've seen.'

'Well *I've* heard of others.' The man pushed his wife away from him. 'Another woman ... two other women. And d'you know why they don't report it? Because they've been going with *them*, that's why.'

The woman began to sob. Leszek put out a hand to her, withdrew it.

'You've been listening to fairy tales.' Rayner lost his temper. 'Is this town going mad, or what? This condition can't be sexually transmitted, so don't punish your wife with your ignorance!' If the woman had not been there he would have added: it may be a symptom of cancer. But instead he said, 'What do you know about disease? Anything at all?' The man was silent. 'Then listen to doctors and not to eyewash.'

33

But the man's bluster concealed an animal fear, he knew. Rayner knew because he felt the same fear, faintly, in himself: an irrational tremor of unease. The discoloration was only a symptom of inner disorder, of course, but the singularity of its deep shade and outline disturbed him as if it were some magic.

The woman was trying to put on her shoes, but in her weakness she could not buckle them. Rayner bent down and helped her. He squeezed her arm. 'It's not a crime to be ill.'

After they had gone, Leszek gazed at him. 'I don't understand.' He lifted the blood sample to the window-light, as if his naked eye might discern something strange. Normally he did not ask Rayner for advice, but now he said, 'What do you think?'

Rayner said brusquely, remembering the reception area full of patients, 'It's probably hormonal.' He suddenly did not want to think about it.

'I don't believe that.' Leszek's face – a landscape of too-thin bones and tissues – was accusing him. 'And you don't think so, really?'

'It's impossible to tell.' Now he was treating Leszek as if his partner had contracted some contagion. Leszek had always been too susceptible, he thought: a taxing mixture of frailty and pride.

Leszek turned away and repeated thinly, 'It's not hormonal.'

Rayner noticed that his head was trembling. But his partner had always been like that, he thought – over-imaginative. Leszek's past, haunted by czarist Russia, had taught him to fear. Years ago, Rayner remembered, Leszek had lent him one of his old suitcases, the battered luggage of his refugee years, and Rayner had seen that it was glazed with shallow scorch-marks. Methodically, scrupulously, Leszek must have burnt away all the labels stuck to it, so that nobody would be able to tell from where he had come.

6

If the town had a heart — and cynics doubted this — it beat in the mall. All the town's nervous sense of purpose, its buoyancy, its latent unease, emanated outwards from this paved half-kilometre of hectic commerce and social rendezvous. Its long bars were always packed. The restaurants flaunted expatriate cuisine, and enfiladed the passing crowds with the lilt of Irish ceilidh or Neapolitan songs. Their names were all of other places: the Vienna Café, the Taj Mahal, London Restaurant, the Temple of Heaven . . . Anywhere but here. Yet here, in the illusion of the town's heart, a practical zeal seemed to unite the marching mass of pedestrians. Even the Babel of immigrant languages had merged into the town's own coarse, quick lingo. Walking by twos and threes, they laughed together. The economy was running high this year. Only when alone, the familiar tension surfaced in their tight mouths and stares.

Nobody looked at the savages perched on their steps and benches, but Rayner knew they no longer went unnoticed. The murders in outlying farms, which had risen to four, had sent an ambiguous frisson through the town — a mixture of fear, half-pleasurable excitement, and underlying anger. Only the natives seemed oblivious of this, and still wandered the streets with their frowns furrowed at something else, and sang their songs at night along the river.

Rayner never walked in the mall without thinking: here I am in the core of the town, and *this is all there is*. The townspeople were so oddly dedicated to their lives, so vigorous and motivated. They had successfully turned their backs on anything but themselves. Sometimes he felt as if he had aged unbearably here. Once or twice, when he could snatch ten minutes from his rounds, he had simply sat in the mall and watched it.

Even in May, with the heat intensifying, the date palms and hibiscus made pools of scent and shadow, and along the benches beneath them an audience of old men in shorts and wide-brimmed hats monitored the bustle. Rayner wondered what they were seeing. They resembled some ancient theatrical chorus. Years of harsh sun had driven the glitter of life deep inside their skulls. In them the town seemed to be watching itself, but with blank eyes.

Rayner snatched his lunch at Nielsen's Baked Potato kiosk, a portable oven rigged up like a caravan. Its cook was a gentle-mannered savage girl (who was to disappear in time), one of the rare natives to have taken work in town. He wanted to ask if people had changed towards her, but instead took his potato in its paper cup and walked away.

In the mall's centre a chess tournament was in progress. Everywhere but here the thoroughfare was paved with small, lava-like blocks, but under the central clump of palms and daturas the black and white paving-slabs formed the board for giant chessmen. Across it the local masters prowled among their wooden pieces as if personally implicated in their fate. But the queens' and knights' faces had been worn away, so the players looked as if they were moving pigs and logs about, and even the spectators were mostly down-at-heel.

Rayner did not know why the back of the woman's head in front of him looked familiar: the dancer's hair seized back into an auburn scallop. Then she turned and he saw Zoë. She accused him laughingly, 'You never stayed for my dance!'

'I did. But I went soon afterwards.' How extraordinary she looked, he thought, flawlessly made up at noon as if she had attended some state function. 'I thought your dance was the only good thing of the evening.'

'Did you?' She sounded tentative now, so that he remembered how girlish she had become when her hair was unloosed. 'You came on a bad night. I didn't dance it well. And there were thugs in the audience.'

The crowd had edged them back against some café tables, mingling them with customers, and Rayner asked her to join him for coffee with a naturalness which vaguely surprised him. The moment they were seated he imagined how incongruous they must look: he so awkward and carelessly dressed, she high-coloured and immaculate. If it were not for the severity of her dancer's hair, he thought, people might have taken her for a high-class prostitute. As it was, she glittered incongruously in the dowdiness, and he sensed that she was enjoying the attention she was drawing – something he didn't like in her.

He said, 'That club must be a tough place to work, isn't it?'

'Yes, but it's a good stage – a deep stage – did you notice? And they let me do what I like . . . probably because they don't care.' She laughed, then said with a sudden, edgy intensity: 'So I choose the music, create the movements, then dance them. It may not seem much, but it's better than what most people get.'

In her voice the lisping cadence peculiar to the capital still mellowed the strident dialect of the town. But this passion for dance, for sheer movement to music, was mysterious to Rayner. Even before he was lamed, he had never danced much.

She said, 'You don't understand, do you? I can tell you don't.' She looked at him, disappointed. 'But that club was better once. We did satire and jazz.'

'Why did you stay on?'

'Why?' She looked as if she had never questioned it. 'I suppose dancing is something I *have* to do. It's the kind of . . . energy – joining the music . . .'

Rayner stared back at her, wondering. He'd never wanted

37

to join the music like that. Music turned him still. To him this woman seemed richly, accusingly young.

'It's just in the body,' she said.

He remembered her body then, how it looked in the outrageous leotard. Even sitting here, she seemed to exist in a unique dimension, at once more precarious and straightforward than his own, and fuller-blooded. The passers-by on the mall evoked a gale of comment and curiosity from her. 'Look at *that* one . . . How do people allow themselves to look like that, d'you think? . . . What a *beautiful* dog, did you see the dog? . . . Now *there's* a good-looking woman . . . Do you play chess? . . . If black doesn't castle he'll lose . . . Oh how extraordinary, *look*! . . .'

Her observations of people – men and women – were openly sensuous. She would admire their legs or necks, their skin colour, the way they walked. And when Arab music sounded from a nearby restaurant, her body began to sway. 'I love that music, don't you?'

Rayner never heard Arab singing without being struck by its exile. It belonged so deeply somewhere else, like the long-faced Syrians in their restaurant. But Zoë seemed to hear and see things in cleansing isolation, enjoying or dismissing them purely for themselves. He started to envy this a little. It was innocently healing. He found himself delighting in her earthiness, her gaiety.

'You should laugh more,' she said suddenly. 'You're getting the wrong lines.'

'What?'

She ran her fingers down his cheeks. 'Your lines are starting to go the wrong way. They're perpendicular.'

He laughed again, and found his fingers momentarily touching her cheekbones.

Hers was, he realised later, a deeply contradictory face. The dancer's immaculacy and vividness most forcefully expressed her, a type of optimism. But beneath the blue compelling eyes and thin nose her mouth twisted up at the corners in a shy assertion of charm. He sat beside her feeling old, but bathed in her exuberance.

'It's too late for me to get smile lines.'

He had paid the bill but realised he did not want to leave. Even in so constricted a town as this, it might be months before he encountered her again. It was not just her beauty which drew him, but her liberating, animal naturalness, and the half-discerned fragility beneath it. She seemed to need him.

So instead of saying, 'I have to go now,' he heard himself ask her, 'How long have you been here?'

'Nearly ten years. I came from the capital.'

'I thought so. Your accent.'

'I wish I could lose it. It sounds so affected.'

Rayner was surprised. 'It's musical. Better than the one here.'

'I prefer the accent here. I find it strong, very emphatic.' She harshened and deepened her words. 'You're from the capital too . . .'

'Yes.'

She was looking at him almost tenderly. 'Did you leave family there?'

'No. My parents were dead when I left. Did you?'

He had no idea what she would answer. She existed so fiercely in her own right that her past was unimaginable. She seemed to live as she herself experienced things – torn up from all associations. He could not envisage her parents. If she had said her father was a factory worker or a government minister, he would not have been surprised.

'My people were schoolteachers from the coast.' She gave a sad laugh, as if acknowledging the incongruity. 'I drove them mad from the start, I was such a rebel. When they got angry, they'd call me "the changeling". Later, I won a scholarship to the dance academy in the capital, and now we don't even exchange letters any more.' She lifted her chin with an odd, hurt self-command. 'There isn't any point.'

He wondered how she had ended up here, but did not like to ask.

She was sitting self-consciously upright now, embattled. 'When I left the academy there weren't many jobs.' She added simply, 'Later I came here.'

Her account – they both knew – resounded with gaps and silences; but he sensed that hers was a past less of scandal than of wilfulness and rebellion, and maybe of political naïvety. She'd simply gone her own way, and had perhaps arrived here by default.

She asked, 'What about you? Are you married?'

He shook his head.

She said, 'I've noticed you before in the streets. You're always on your own.'

'I'm a doctor.'

'Yes, I know . . .' She was not flirting with him, but he wondered what had elicited this tinge of condolence. What did he look like in the streets? Just overworked, he imagined. But occasionally he had caught sight of himself in a shop mirror – taking his reflection by surprise – and had glimpsed a face more gaunt and hard than the one he had reckoned on.

Zoë said astonishingly, 'You don't look happy.' Her accent had slid back into the lilt of the capital.

'Happy?' He burst into contradictory laughter. 'Yes, I'm happy sometimes, when I'm not thinking about it. On a good day, I'm happy working.' He glanced at his watch. He was already ten minutes late.

But it was hard – ludicrously hard – to let this woman go, just to say, 'Goodbye, then,' and to carry on. His own indecision surprised him. His hands were toying with the tablecloth. Then he and Zoë stood up together.

He said, 'Come and have supper one evening after you've finished dancing.'

She looked momentarily surprised, and for another instant gazed at him rather gravely, as if assessing something. Then she said, 'I'd like that.'

7

The road to the wilderness crossed the river and passed through the mines. Among their discoloured slag heaps the wheels of the winder-houses turned in slow motion, and above them, from a stack fifty metres up in the sky, the smoke from the smelter plant unfurled a long, black banner over the town. Then the installations dwindled through a slovenly amphitheatre of hills, where a narrow-gauge railway trailed over mineral pinks and greys.

The road held the plume of smoke in view for ten kilometres into the wilderness. The car wheels lisped over tarmac and a film of sand. Recently, whenever he could find time, Rayner had taken to driving alone into this emptiness: a savannah of stunted acacia and whitened grass whirring with cicadas. He felt eased here. It was a kind of shriving. All the vehemence and frustration of the town seemed to dissipate without hiatus into the empty circle of the horizon. The grey-red earth was soft, cracked, and the sky hung unchanging: a land without purpose or memory. It put him at peace.

Once he passed a shrunken water-hole where some natives were grazing their cattle. Their bullocks' haunches stuck out like knives. He lifted his hand in greeting, but they only stared. Beyond, the grasslands merged again into the plains, spiked with saltbush and desert oaks. There was no wind. The leaves hung limp, and the steppe ran to the sky like a faded carpet.

On his old War Ministry map a dotted line led to a faded asterisk, the site of native rock-paintings. Two of the older

41

townsmen had faintly remembered seeing them, sheltered in a hollow. But for years nobody had been there. Leszek, who had visited them as a youth almost fifty years ago, could not remember what they depicted. He'd only said, 'You can't go there now, surely? To one of the savages' places? Oh no, not after what's been happening . . . They'd kill you.'

'It's deserted, isn't it?'

'I don't remember. With the savages you can't always tell . . .'

In the end Rayner had resorted to a book written forty years earlier by a missionary who had tried to convert the elusive wilderness tribes. It pinpointed the site thirty-two kilometres south-east of the town: 'a rocky hollow, still a shrine of the local tribespeople. Its paintings are crude and much faded . . .'

The tarmac road had dwindled to sand long before another track – no wider than a footpath – bifurcated to the east. Rayner followed it gingerly over the hardened ground. It seemed to go on for a long time. Once or twice, where the earth lightened, he thought he was approaching cornfields, but they resolved into faded grass on a faded earth.

Then the track stopped dead. The hollow opened so abruptly beneath him that only the sudden green of its treetops gave warning. It was small, circular – an eccentric dimple in the plain. It looked like what it could not be: the mouth of a buried volcano.

He peered over the edge. The place seemed empty. A few gum trees lifted from the dust. A depleted water-hole stared from its grass like a sunken eye. The heat had grown intense. Rayner scrambled down and began to circle the hollow. Sometimes the soft earth had dropped from its banks to show scarps of schist-like rock. He scrutinised their surfaces for paintings, but found none. Only at the base of one he was surprised to come upon a bowl of plaited cane filled with withered berries. Laid on twigs at the foot of the rock-face, it must have been somebody's tribute or thanksgiving. But to whom? The scarp showed nothing.

But as he examined it, there arose a deep, reverberant *Oyohoyoh*! It was so muffled that at first he imagined it came from somewhere above him or even from the rock.

Oyohoyo!

Then Rayner saw them, a pair of savages – an old man and a girl – watching him from the gum trees. He could not tell if the shout had been welcome or warning. They did not move. They seemed as uncertain as he was.

He raised his hand in greeting, and the old man lifted both his in reply. Rayner had not noticed the conical hut sheltered against one cliff. The pair watched him coming. He had not bargained for this. Mentally he had dissociated the holy place (if that is what it was) from the people who had worshipped here, as if he were visiting somewhere long dead, a property of the wilderness. But now the townsman's fear surfaced in him: a tingle of revulsion and alarm. In the half-minute that he took to reach the natives, the axed-in heads came floating against his shins again.

As Rayner reached him, he saw an old man of barbarian majesty. He wore a shabby pair of trousers rolled up at the ankles, and was clasping a flimsy stick. He looked huge. His flaccid shoulders and torso, dusted in grey hair, sloped without interruption into passive arms and stomach, before slipping away towards the delicate feet and hands of all this people. And his face was extraordinary. It nested in a tumult of hair and beard, as if he were staring from grey flames. Under their overhung brows the eyes were nearly invisible – Rayner couldn't even see their whites – but his skin glittered an igneous blue-black, as though its pigment had turned mineral.

The girl stood behind him in a torn white dress and a necklace of seeds. She looked about eighteen. The extremities of her hair had been twisted to ginger rat's-tails.

Rayner said, 'I hope it's right my coming here.' He did

43

not even know if they spoke his language. 'I thought it was empty.'

'Is empty,' the man said gruffly. 'You go where you like, but go careful. Is blackfeller place, but okay you look.'

He turned and said something to the girl. She ran forward and held out a wooden mixing-dish filled with yams. He took one, and she darted back. She might have been the old man's wife or granddaughter, it was impossible to tell. Only her bird-like movements expressed her. Her face looked blank, except for the savage's expression of distant puzzlement.

Rayner said, 'Are you living here alone? Are you the guardian?'

'We just living with our living,' the man said. 'But this like whitefeller say, retirement job. This old feller's job.' He gazed at Rayner as if at a landscape, impassively, through his overcast eyes. 'But sometimes we go into town too, buy trousers, buy shoes, buy the other things.'

Rayner's unease had gradually merged into curiosity. Because these people were not of the town, he found an obscure release in them. Even the shabbiness of the savages was interesting, because it was not the town's shabbiness. 'You speak our language.'

'I got the stock-farmers' language, you know, worked for three, four years, fencing and yarding. Big farm downriver. Bloke by the name Ellis. You know Ellis? But I like to keep one place now. I can't throw the bullocks no more.' He swept out one arm in an arc. 'Living is all right till a feller gets old. So I stay here now and look after the places.'

'What places?' Rayner asked. 'Painted places?'

'Ancestors,' the man said. 'I can show you ancestors. There not many to see, eh, but I show you. Some of them gone now, is gone by rain and wind, and some. But most is staying, not too much.'

He lumbered over to the scarp that Rayner had just left,

moving with a leaden, broken gait which suddenly reduced him. Then he stood in front of the rock-face. 'You see them?'

But Rayner saw nothing. Over the surface spread a web of hairline fissures, and the confusion of colours between them looked like blemishes of the living rock. The old man struck his hip. 'You come stand here. Look now. Is different shadow, eh?' Rayner went and stood by him. The man pointed with his stick. 'See there . . . there?'

Rayner looked again. And before his eyes, the figures awakened out of the stone. The whole surface lit up into new patterns: hunters, warriors, women, herders . . . He was astonished that he had not discerned them before.

'Now you see.'

The figures were elongated and graceful. They floated in random patterns across the rock. Where its face had flaked away, they left amputated legs or heads. Rayner could make out a hunting party pursuing the miniature gazelles of the wilderness; a line of men on the march; a circle of women who seemed to be talking or preparing food; and higher up, where the pigment had oxidised and half gone, a phantom battle raged.

He asked in amazement, 'How did they get these colours?' Some of the tones looked unfaded: white, yellow and blood red.

The man said: 'They opened stones.'

The artists, Rayner guessed, had used pigments of charcoal and pipeclay and the ochreous local ironstone. The images were all in silhouette: incarnate shape and movement. They appeared less like people than ideas of people. Even when fighting, they seemed to be engaged in an aerial ballet.

He asked, 'What kind of men painted these?'

The old savage thought a while before answering. 'Priests.'

Rayner had no idea what the paintings were trying to

do. They portrayed everyday life – but as if it were paradise. He could not resist the idea that they contained some secret, something known also to the savages sitting motionless on the town steps, gazing into an inner distance. But knowing how compulsively he laid his own ideas on neutral things, he asked, 'Are these life without the white man?'

The old man encircled the paintings with a wide flourish of his stick. 'This life our people always. This is life after the tree come down.'

'Tree?'

The man pointed at what appeared to be a white river wavering between the paintings. 'The tree come down. Who brings it down? Maybe some devil bring it down, maybe the people from the other place, the salt marsh people, I don't know. But it got cut and there's no more climbing up and down, only the sky like you see. This is the story now.'

Rayner wondered if the savage was confusing him on purpose. Perhaps he had enquired too closely. And now the man was pointing to the far side of the imaginary tree, tracing a surface whose paintings looked fainter and older. 'Is the time before Time.'

In this bleached space, animals were the same size as men. They seemed to inhabit a region without gravity, and a few were upside down. Hare, lizard, human, antelope – they floated together in stressless equality. Some of their heads were turned, as though they held conversation. But compared with the other figures they looked full-blown, static, as if they had reached completion or perhaps not begun. Hunters froze by their spears. Animals just sat.

The savage said, 'This is happiness.'

Even the dancers described only hieroglyphs of dance, with their hands raised hieratically above their heads – although the loosened pose of one woman reminded

46

Rayner bizarrely of Zoë, who had slept last night in his arms.

The man said, 'The animals painted in their own blood. Gazelle is in gazelle blood, hare is in hare blood. That's how they painted, eh.' The native was now breathing audibly, and Rayner noticed that he was starting to sweat. 'Maybe these things painted by God.'

Rayner stepped back in frustration, to view the whole rock-face from a distance. He felt he was gazing, illiterate, at a crucial text. It seemed to portray a felicity from which the white man had been excluded at some primordial time: a kind of lost knowledge. And the savage could only explain it in riddles. But if this was the inner world which these people inhabited, Rayner thought, why did they axe people's heads in?

He asked, 'What is this tree?'

'This tree, I not seen it since I was young.' The man flung out one arm towards the south. 'Those people not my clan.'

Rayner looked foolishly to where he pointed. 'What people? Where?'

'Out there, I don't remember how far. Maybe five days away, maybe ten. I don't know. They're not my people, like I say. But most blackfellers been there one time or other. Tree place is like the world's middle, eh.' He touched his stomach-button. 'The navel of the world.'

Strange how many people imagined they lived at the centre of the world, Rayner thought, while for him it was always somewhere else.

The savage turned and started back heavily towards the hut. Rayner said quickly, 'May I use a camera?'

'Camera?'

'Yes.' He took it from its case.

The old man frowned at it. 'What does this do?'

'It makes pictures of things.' Cameras were commonplace in the town now.

The savage took the black box delicately in his hands, and

47

peered into the lens. His forehead had depressed into inky corrugations. He handed it back. 'You show me.'

Rayner pointed the box along the cliff-face. He had left its hood and tripod in the car. The old man listened to its clicking and waited for something to happen. After Rayner had finished he asked, 'Where is the painting?'

'The painting is in the camera. They take it out in the town.'

He was not sure if the man believed him. They walked back slowly to the hut. It looked makeshift: just myrtle boughs and straw. Behind it, sprinkled with chips of painted bark, was a fresh grave. The girl was cooking outside, but jumped up as they approached, and pulled some grass-seed cakes from the ashes. The man said, 'My daughter has made you welcome-cakes.' They sat down opposite one another, and he broke one. The girl disappeared into the hut, and after a while Rayner heard the clacking of a loom.

The old man started cramming the bread into his mouth. He said, 'I heard some blokes been making trouble round town area.'

'There've been murders in the outlying farms. You heard that?'

'Yes, I heard that. These bad fellers make like they get rid of white man. One bad bloke makes it wrong for all of us. They grow angry because no rain. They go a little out of their heads. That's how it takes them, the drought. Is hard if rains don't come and cattle all dying, one there, one here, dying.'

'The people in town are getting angry too,' Rayner said. 'They think *they* live at the earth's centre!'

The man did not understand. 'That's another place, the earth's centre, long way south.' He extended his arm again. Rayner saw that he was shaking slightly, his whole body shaking. He kept ramming his stick in and out of the embers, as if to raise heat. His breathing had become a sad, nasal sighing. He said, 'But that tree cut now. Nobody climbs up and down no more. It's just sky now.' He pulled his stick from the cinders and inscribed something in the dust. 'That's the tree now.'

As his stick withdrew, Rayner saw that he had outlined a tall stump, like a phallus: some early object of worship, perhaps. But even in the crude medium of dust, his shaking hand had invested it with nervous, quivering lines.

Rayner said, 'Are you feeling unwell?'

'I get bad from the hot heat.' The man spread his hand over his chest. 'And sometimes in my left eye, if I looking at my hand, I see two hands, one top, one bottom.' He did not try this. 'But I'm okay most days. My daughter gets medicine grass and sometimes whitefeller stuff. I've been lucky in my living, not like some.'

He became silent. Rayner went on hearing the clack-clack of the loom. Through the hut opening, beyond the girl's back, he glimpsed their possessions: a skin rug, some articles of western clothing, and in the centre, incongruously beautiful, the carved headrests on which these mysterious people slept. At the girl's feet were a few bowls of roots and tubers, and a little beyond, exorcised of any threat, a short-handled axe.

Rayner wondered what the girl would do after her father had died. He badly wanted to give them something. He felt suddenly, illogically grateful to them – simply for their difference, their enigma. But as he got to his feet he realised he had nothing useful to give.

He took the old man's arm. 'Next time you're in the town, you come and see me. I'm a doctor.' He printed out his address on a scrap of paper. 'You show this to people, they'll tell you where to come.'

The man laid the paper flat on the palm of his hand, then turned without a word into the hut.

Rayner scrambled up the slope to his car. It was already dusk. The wilderness seemed to be sucking the light out of the sky. As he drove back, the lamps of the mines ascended in front of him in constellations of white and amber, and the mammoth smelting chimney, picked out in red against the stars, still spread its waste in a long, fine dust across the night.

8

Rayner found himself saying things to Zoë which he had never intended. Often when they were together her stare fell on him like a vivid but innocent searchlight, and he was touched by a kind of impetuous tenderness. They had slept with one another after only their second evening together, and within two weeks, a little bewildered at himself, he had asked her to join him on holiday. It was the animal exuberance of her, he thought, which was so elating, mixed with an intangible sense of suffering. Her vitality struck him as a kind of courage. For all her frankness, he felt he did not know her.

He chose the town's most sophisticated resort – a lake in the northern hills – because he imagined that she was urban. But during their few days' holiday neither of them entered the little casino or nightclub, and it was she who sank into a dream by the water, and seemed physically to imbibe its colours and changes. For hours she would paddle along the shore in one of his shirts and a straw hat, then lie spreadeagled on a rock under the flailing sun, with her hair swept over her face. She said that it reminded her of home, and certainly the lake was so huge – on hazy days the farther shore vanished altogether – that it resembled some tideless stretch of the north coast where she was born.

There was nothing like it for hundreds of kilometres. Through the naked hills it lay in a sheet of brilliant blue, death-still. Under its near slopes, fed by small streams, the littoral burst into a rain-forest of mangrove and silkwood trees, where parasite ferns ran amok and hundreds of pale trunks leant askew. The resort's villas were nestled privately among them along a near-empty beach. Even in June it was silent. Out on the water only a few transparent-looking islands interposed themselves between the shore and the far hills, and occasional flights of duck gashed the surface.

Rayner usually avoided such resorts. During the Great War the place had been reserved for the local government élite and senior army and intelligence officers. Now it was patronised by executives and businessmen. After a day dispersed along the shore or among the islands, they converged on the dining-room with their wives or mistresses, and the place became a microcosm of the town. It drank and danced and gossiped. To Rayner, who couldn't dance and scarcely drank, all the place's pleasure lay in Zoë. If any medical colleagues happened to be here, he decided, they could think what they liked. He was not ashamed of her. He felt proud, rather, of her public face: the slightly arrogant beauty of her, which seemed to be defying the world to uncover any weaker woman beneath. People in the town were so various now – the strata of the old society breaking up all over the country – that you'd expect nobody to trouble any longer about who consorted with whom. But you would, of course, be wrong. And the dining-room by the lake was riddled with a cross-fire of stares and inquisition.

So at evening, after their amphibious hours along the shore, they had to reenter the town's orbit. Zoë prepared for this as if she were going to war. Sitting at her dressing-table, applying her fawn-coloured foundation-cream and diffusing over her eyelids the specks of rouge which mysteriously heightened her eyes' blue, she talked about creating her face as if none had been there before. Then came the matching lipstick and the small false eyelashes and the drawing-back of the hair from her highlit features. Without this, Rayner came to realise, she felt bared, whittled away. So each night she produced a version of herself which was at once emphatic, theatrical and a little poignant. He was reminded of the dancer who had gyrated on the nightclub stage, demanding recognition of herself, but only on her own terms.

'Do I look all right? I think I look a mess.' In the long mirror the girl could not decide, turned to Rayner.

'You look good.'

Then her chin lifted and she walked down the plant-lapped path to the dining-room with a trace still of the ballerina's turned-out step, and her hand on Rayner's arm. As they threaded between tables towards one overlooking the lake, and people turned to assess them, Rayner felt bemused that her fear of crowds and her defiance of them went hand in hand. Her way of coping was to recreate herself for them. It seemed neurotically brave.

A three-piece orchestra was playing Glinka and Borodin on a dais, and a few couples were dancing. The women's hair was stuck with the little gold combs fashionable that year. The men's white dinner jackets were buttoned tight at the waist, and a few were still stitched with campaign ribbons from the Great War twenty years ago, when the nation was a colony.

Already Zoë's high spirits were discovering a humorous variety show in the people near them when somebody called out, 'Rayner!'

Her heart must have sunk as his did. She said, 'Oh bloody hell. It's Ivar and Felicie.'

They were sitting alone at a table for four, wanting company. Ivar spread out his arms in amused welcome. At that moment his urbanity, his inability to be surprised by human affairs, came as a relief. He merely kissed them both perfunctorily and said, 'How good to find friends!'

But Felicie flung her arms furiously around Zoë. 'You cheat! You didn't *tell* me.' She turned to Ivar. 'She tells me she needs a holiday but never says *where* or *who with*.'

'You never listen,' said Zoë.

Felicie said, 'But I'd have listened to *that*!'

So they settled at the table and lapsed into the ease of old friends. Their meal came and went, and they were left drinking the rough local wine from the hills. Rayner felt happy, and for the first time in years he drank too much. Felicie poured out news at Zoë as if they'd been parted six months, telling anecdotes, soliciting approval, and scattering all her chatter with reflex self-criticism. 'I'm so forgetful, I . . . I'm so stupid, I . . . I . . .' Her voice fluted and piped. Rayner, watching from the corner of his eye, found the two laughably different. Mist-haired Felicie gave an illusion almost of transparency, while beside her Zoë was all colour and bite. Several times it occurred to him that Felicie was some sort of ghost. In her irrecoverable loss of self, he thought, she was the person whom Zoë was refusing to become.

Ivar was saying, 'I thought they'd have wanted you in town now.'

'You mean the disease?' Rayner shook his head. 'We can't treat it. We can pretend, of course, we always do. But basically we don't know anything.'

Ivar said levelly, 'You'll be able to track it down in the end. How many cases are reported now? Eleven?'

'We'd be able to trace it better if we knew what it was. But we've taken blood and urine tests and come up with nothing at all. We've even X-rayed for cancer, but . . . nothing.'

'You think it's infectious?'

'I don't know. Nothing's shown up in the blood.'

He said, 'Well then, the people who've caught it can be monitored. There must be some common factor.'

'They're all sorts. Both sexes, old, young. Two are miners, One's an optician. A bank clerk . . .' The school medical officer – Rayner's amateur analyst – had even reported the rash on a child of six.

Ivar said, 'How strange,' but he said it reluctantly,

acknowledging only a temporary barrier which would soon be cleared away. That was typical, Rayner thought. Ivar had always spread this calm of logic and reasonableness about him, which left no place for the unknown. Now he added, 'People say it's a savage's disease — even that they're spreading it on purpose.'

'There's no evidence for that!' It was maddening, Rayner thought, how Ivar could voice a piece of pure speculation, and in his measured tone the idea would take on sanity. Whereas Rayner, when he refuted it, sounded harshly precarious.

Ivar said, 'I'd have thought it permissible, under the circumstances, to take in a few of the local savages for medical inspection.'

'It'd be harder to diagnose in natives than in anybody.' Rayner remembered the blotched torso of the old man at the holy site. 'I think they generally suffer the opposite complaint. Skin depigmentation. And apart from discoloration the only symptoms are vague. Just a general malaise. And some patients complain of aching eyeballs.'

'Did you know,' Ivar said, 'that during the last savage troubles fourteen years ago they systematically poisoned the town's water supply?'

'I never heard that.'

'Well, they did — '

Felicie broke in, 'Ivar thinks the savages are "racially inferior".' Her head wobbled like a flower. 'Do *you*?'

Rayner laughed (it seemed the only thing to do). 'Genetics isn't my subject.' But when he thought about the natives, he felt a confused disquiet. Between them and the whites there seemed to lie some absolute divide, as if they inhabited another stratum of time. He said, 'I suppose they're inferior when they've had to adapt to our way. We'd be, if we had to adapt to theirs.'

He did not want to talk about it. Through a window behind Ivar's back he saw that the moon had risen out of the hills. He wrenched himself to his feet and walked out onto the terrace. The wine had gone to his head. In front of him only the lake and the moon seemed to exist in the simplifying night. He even fancied that this was where the moon came from, out of the lake. He was reminded of the sea coast near the capital on other summer nights, of Miriam, of phosphorus water in the rock-pools. The restaurants in the capital, he thought, did not have to strain for effect as this one did, with its pretentious chandeliers and fake leather upholstery.

Ivar had followed him out. 'Felicie wasn't joking,' he said. 'I do think that. These people are radically different. You only have to look at the shape of their heads to see it. There simply isn't enough room for a developed neo-cortex.'

Rayner chilled. Ivar, he'd noticed, was reading a manual called *Leadership Effectiveness*. He seemed to be mentally arming himself. To Ivar, knowledge must always have a purpose – Rayner remembered this from their schooldays. Everything was used, directed to an end. Nothing existed simply for itself.

Rayner said, 'It's not as simple as that.'

Ivar answered quite affectionately, 'You always did complicate things.' He dropped his cigarette stub over the verandah. 'But just look at Felicie's head-shape, for example. That's the brain case of a sheep.'

'Are you joking?'

'Not in the least.' But he laughed. 'This is the last holiday she and I take together. She's an exceptionally pretty woman, don't you think, but there's too much I dislike in her, and I've no doubt she'd say the same about me.'

'There's something desperate about her.'

'I'll keep an eye on her after we've split up.'

Rayner watched Ivar's face in the moonlight: the putty-like face in which nothing was memorable, except the bland balance of the whole. Yes, Ivar would keep an eye on Felicie. Rayner's childhood memories of him were all of a

56

premature adult, mocking a little, but kindly within limits: a man to whom cruelty would be a waste of energy.

He went on gazing at the moonstruck lake. His head was clearing, but not happily. If he had not known Ivar in childhood, he thought, they could never have become friends. Yet sometimes he felt irritated at his own inability to embrace life as Ivar did. Everything seemed to grate on him harder than on others – on these robust townspeople drinking and dancing behind him, their exile forgotten. Ivar and the town were right for one another, he thought. They were all ruled by a merciless common sense: whether in accepting a theory about the savages' inferiority (one of God's slips, they would say) or the lot of the pathetic Felicie.

'Zoë will help her,' Rayner said. 'I think she relies on Zoë.'

'Yes, she probably does.' Ivar turned quiet. 'But you can't rely on Zoë except in bursts.' He took Rayner's arm, asserting their old friendship, its primacy over any later ones. 'I've known Zoë several years, and she's very self-willed, complex . . . She's a solitary.'

Perhaps Ivar was warning him against falling in love. But in some way, Rayner thought, Zoë had offended him.

'Don't misunderstand me,' he went on. 'She's good-looking, she's intelligent . . . On a six-day holiday she'll be fine.' He gave a collusive laugh. 'But then, she's never the same . . .'

It was the first time Rayner had seen this look on Ivar's face: perplexity. So he had failed to understand her.

Then Rayner felt a sudden distaste at them both standing here, talking about their temporary women. He did not want to discuss Zoë any longer. But he could not resist asking, 'How the hell did she land up in this town?'

'She's always gone her own way. Her parents are decent people in the north, you know. Teachers. But she had to be different . . .'

Zoë and Felicie came out onto the terrace then, exclaiming

at the moonlight and the men's absence. They had twined jasmine in each other's hair. Their laughter tinkled in the night. Anyone boating on the lake, Rayner thought, would have seen two glamorous young women carelessly on holiday with their men . . .

Behind them the band had struck up one of the syncopated dance tunes popular that year. In front, an isolated wind was interfering with the moonlight all over the lake. Felicie was walking unsteadily up and down the terrace, crooning to herself. Zoë, standing close to Rayner, had started listening for owls, and he was conscious of her hands resting beside him on the verandah stonework, their long fingers interlaced. Ivar came and stood beside them, his jacket hung carelessly over his arm.

Then Ivar reached out and covered Zoë's hands with one of his. It was a broad hand, Rayner saw. A gold ring glinted on it. Ivar said, 'Come and dance.'

There was something so assured, so proprietorial about the gesture, that Zoë's reaction was the more shocking. Her hands darted from under his and bunched whitely at her waist. For a split second an abyss of vulnerability opened up in her. Then her anger covered her. For an instant Rayner saw her eyes flash down at his crippled foot, the one which could not dance, then up again at Ivar. Her hands were behind her back. She breathed, '*No*!'

Because he scarcely knew her, her character splintered with awesome complexity before his eyes. Every night she would wipe away with cold cream the elaborate evening face she had composed, and there would appear beneath it her other, softer persona. With her hair loosed behind her back like a young girl's, her features appeared thinner, peakier. Even the lustre in her eyes seemed to change. It calmed to a tentative stare. Her whole demeanour seemed to be asking: am I all right?

58

This changed person awoke Rayner's protectiveness. It was as if this capacity in him – a kind of impassioned tenderness – had been there long ago, waiting for her. At night the slender dancer's arms with their elongated fingers twined about him in blind urgency, so that he wanted to calm her into himself. Yet whenever he started to think that this orphan was her only manifestation, its mirror-image would erupt – vital, playful, defiant – and she would revert to her daytime self: the owner of the proud back and strong-shaped legs. Then she would tease and laugh at him and at herself, like somebody watching a carnival.

He sensed that she carried with her a past as disjoined as his own. At first, because she didn't refer to it, he thought her secretive. Then he realised that she just wanted to forget: she despised self-pity. For years after leaving the capital she had lived hand-to-mouth, performing in theatre and cabaret. She had started to drink too much; and yes, there had been many men.

She spoke without regret. She wanted him to know. After leaving dance academy, she said, she might have entered the state ballet company. But she'd fallen in love with jazz and flamenco, and joined a mime theatre instead. 'Everybody said I was mad, because we were openly political. Our director behaved as if the country was as free as it pretended to be, and we did shows about every state farce and corruption.' She laughed ruefully. 'But we were just children, of course, trying to make the world all right.'

Rayner wondered in astonishment how this little theatre had survived in the twenties, when censorship in the capital had been as harsh as during the war. But within a year, she said, they were all being persecuted. She had been living with one of the actors and become pregnant, when they were denounced to the authorities. She was warned that unmarried motherhood was an abuse to the state. Her parents refused to see her again unless she agreed to an abortion.

'But I could feel the baby already alive in me.' Her voice emptied of any tone, as if against weeping. At eight months she had given birth to a stillborn boy, and for an instant had held him in her hands, and seen his expression.

She detached Rayner's arms from her, as if they could not comfort. After a while, with sudden, bitter humour, she said: 'In the puritan crackdown I got reassigned to other work. Dancers like me were listed Grade Seven, along with prostitutes and gypsies. I was told to start clerical training.'

'Did you?'

'No. I said I'd rather lose my residence permit than stop dancing. So I was reassigned here.' She added grimly, brutalising herself. 'Basically, I was chucked out.'

Her honesty, especially when turned on herself, sounded almost callous. He cupped her face in his hands and kissed her. He did not understand this obscure battle to dance.

But four years ago, she said, for no reason she knew, her suffering – this shadow-boxing with herself and with authority – had eased. She had stopped drinking. She had started living alone, and had adopted the discipline of yoga. Once she tried to explain this to him, but only ended in confusion. 'We're getting into deep water!'

But every afternoon by the lake she would disappear for an hour. The shoreline was littered with flat, seal-grey rocks belted with the marks of seasonal evaporation, and on one of these she would settle, facing the sun. Then her prayer-like stretchings and bendings would begin, the private suppleness which would bring her feet close against her breast or arch them behind her back. She doubled and twisted, did headstands and shoulder-stands or balanced with one leg behind her neck, all in a rhythmic, concentrated calm.

Meanwhile he swam or lay reading, and watched the wind chafe or polish the lake surface, while often the far shore stood invisible in haze, as if this were indeed the ocean of their childhood memory. But in fact its water rested tideless against the rocks, and its mood and beauty were beginning to depend on her. Her sudden fervours and withdrawals were starting to obsess him. In conversation she poured questions over him – straightforward but demanding ones about anything she didn't know – with that disturbing innocence of hers. She would listen to him with an almost anguished attention, which would then fade for no reason he could guess, and suddenly return.

Even in bed she often clasped him with an impassioned, hurt need, as if she had nothing else in the world, and when she stared at him he felt her pulling out love through his eyes, scouring his skull clean. So he made love to her in a euphoria of longing, tinged with sorrow. Yet at other times, as if from years of wounding, she would show only a detached affection; then she seemed to be holding back some vital part of her, and proving to herself, with a raw sadness, that she was, after all, separate. Once, sensing this, he asked, 'Do you want me to go to sleep?' – and she nodded, filling him with a pang of intense, hopeless separation.

Now in the morning, when he lay idle on the lake's verge, the offshore islands seemed to rage or go melancholy, depending on the night before. In some way, he realised, he had fallen in love with her.

But just as she incarnated two different women, so she demanded two men of him. The man who intrigued her with conversation during the day – 'my pet brain' – was not allowed to possess her at night. For this she turned him into someone else. For a while her gaze would drain him and her body would cling, as if they might complete one another. Then she would say, 'Don't talk. Just love me,' and close her eyes. She wanted him both as lover and friend, but the two could not, in the end, overlap. The man who entered her had to be a stranger.

Once, watching her writhe in his arms as if in some

61

private trance, he said bemusedly, 'I might as well be a stud.'

Her eyes opened in distress. 'No ... no. It's not important.'

'What isn't?'

'Sex.' She looked shy, as if she had just focused him. 'I've never really wanted sex.'

He drew back from her, astonished. He'd believed her more erotic than him. She'd had affairs since she was sixteen.

She said, 'I've only wanted male companionship, in the end. That's why I went wild as a girl. I just wanted to be held.'

She shot him a depleted smile. Suddenly, staring down at her, he imagined all the men in whose carnal energies she had looked for love – including, perhaps, his own – and felt sick with pity.

But she saw his expression and started to laugh. 'Don't look like that. Christ! I was using them too. I wasn't so badly treated, except by Ivar.'

'I wanted to ask about that.'

So they sat up against the pillows in one another's arms, and talked about Ivar. She tilted her head a little away, as if freeing herself to judge or remember, but her words came in bursts of self-contempt.

'I should have known it'd be no good. He and his army friends had been picking girls up at the club for nearly a year, and I thought I had his measure.' She still sounded angry. 'Then, out of nowhere, I fell in love with him. It's the only time it's happened to me like that. He'd been trying to get me for months, and one morning I just woke up knowing, "I love him".' She gave a disdainful laugh. 'But it wasn't for long. Three months, I think.'

Rayner thought he could guess Ivar's allure for women: the malleable face, quite sensual in its softness, which could deploy expressions by remote control and was, in its way, perfectly sincere.

Zoë said, 'But he's cold at heart, Ivar. Dead. He doesn't want a woman, he wants a servant. There's something in him . . . something . . . not there at all. So he humiliates you. You go mad for him and he stays utterly sane.'

'Why were you so hurt?'

She said, 'Just that he didn't care.' Her look of depletion returned. Her fingers kneaded his. 'He treated love as a kind of . . . eccentricity. Women don't really exist for him, you know. Not as people. He thinks he likes intelligent women, but he doesn't. He doesn't like stupid ones either. Poor Felicie.'

Rayner felt a stab of jealousy. He turned and lifted Zoë against him. Her body had turned cool with the night.

'I don't want to feel that ever again,' she said, as if guessing his sadness. 'You're better than he is.'

She closed her mouth over his to stop it talking, and for long minutes Rayner gave up thinking as he moved with the rhythm of the soft, schizophrenic body under his. Only later, as she clung to him with what might have been gratitude, and sighed a little, did he remember the man he couldn't be for her, and his jealousy returned. In exchange for her deep, helpless commitment, he knew, he would have given up all that he elicited in respect and affection. Like Ivar, he thought uneasily, he wanted to own her.

The weather held until their last day. Then the haze which had lain all week over the lake bloomed malignantly to suffocate the sky, and the sun disappeared. It felt like the stifling prelude to a storm – which never came.

Without the sun, time vanished. Rayner swam with closed eyes where the shore steepened under canopies of trees. His slow breaststrokes parted a flotsam of rotted coconut husks and palm leaves. He thought about Ivar:

how most people must seem mad to him. Zoë had simmered under his calm for a while, then surfaced to baffle him, baffle herself. He could not imagine them together.

He shuddered as something brushed under his feet: something soft. But gazing down through the peat-coloured water, he saw only a decayed silkwood trunk. His nerves were frayed, he thought. One week's holiday was too little. He swam to one of the island rocks which looked smooth but were rough and cutting, and heaved himself up.

Around a bend in the shore, bobbing under a magenta bathing-cap, came Felicie. Soon she was swimming around his rock, chatting. The sun had turned her shoulders pink.

'Where's Zoë?'

'Practising her yoga.'

'Oh how could she?' She steadied herself beside the rock. 'All that twisting about. It looks so *ugly*. It's not natural.'

'Where's Ivar?'

'Reading.' She squirmed onto the ledge below him. 'That's all he ever does, apart from . . . God it's so boring here. What do you do all day?'

She glanced down at her feet in the water. She craved excitement, change. But instead there was just Ivar, who would not change, and herself. It was all very well for Zoë, she said, Zoë was never bored. In fact Zoë couldn't keep still for more than a cigarette. She must be tiring to live with. 'Isn't she?' There was open coquetry in the question.

Rayner said, 'You know her.' It was probably futile to hunt for clues to Zoë in the muddled memory of Felicie, but he heard himself add, 'Has she always been like that?'

'Oh yes, even three years ago with Ivar. Christ, she led him a dance. Served him right. She was the only woman to *walk out* on him.' Felicie levered herself up the rock beside Rayner. 'Zoë goes *mad* sometimes. She takes everything too hard.' Her slim legs were burnt prawn pink. 'I'm the steady one.'

But nobody looked less steady than Felicie, Rayner

thought. Her mouth, turned slackly to his, was pleading to be kissed. It was not a planned betrayal, just the moment's need. Now that Ivar was drifting from her, she would cling to whatever floated.

Rayner said, 'Zoë and Ivar would never have got on.'

Felicie look away. 'I suppose Ivar's never changed either, has he?' Her words pattered with despair.

'No.'

Abruptly she got up and said, 'I'd better go back,' then added as if recanting something, 'Give my love to Zoë!'

Ridiculous and touching in the magenta bathing-cap, she eased into the water and started to return the way she had come.

After a while Rayner too swam to the shore. His damaged foot had started to ache, throbbing as if the bone marrow were filled with nerves. He lay down and heaped the soft earth into a cushion beneath it. When Zoë found him, he was fast asleep.

'Are you all right?'

'Yes.'

She stood gazing down at him. She looked as he most loved her to look. From time to time, as now, something ignited in her this glow of tenderness. Even at meals, she might reach out with a sensitivity strange after her withdrawal, and cup his face in her hands to steady it, before settling to gaze at him. So now her eyes had gone gentle and alert, and she sat down and tentatively touched his foot. So that was it: his foot.

She said, 'You never talk about it, so I don't know when it's hurting.'

'I don't think about it much.'

She ran her fingertips over the permanently swollen ankle. 'But it must remind you.'

'Yes, of course it does.' Some roughness reentered his voice. 'I don't mean it reminds me of the accident. I had amnesia. But it reminds me of my mother's death. It's like carrying it about with you.' And the end of your youth too, he thought angrily, and your exile to this bloody place. 'You imagine that if it wasn't there, you'd forget.' But of course you wouldn't, he knew. He sat up and stared down his body with distaste. 'Zoë, you and I should have a pact to ban pity.'

She said, 'Why should we be frightened of it, d'you suppose?' She lifted his wrenched foot to her lips. Its bones stuck out like harp strings. She kissed them one by one.

He said, 'I'm not frightened.'

She answered astonishingly, 'I am.' Her fingers trickled over his foot. 'If I thought you were sorry for me, I'd start to feel pitiful. Then I'd lose myself.'

In the sunless day the only sign of dusk was an overall dimming, as if a great lamp had been turned down behind the sky.

She said, 'We should go soon.'

They wandered back to dress for supper. Zoë remade her face. When it was done, she went on glaring longer than usual into the mirror, hunting for any fissures in her immaculacy. Rayner studied her, wondering; he wanted to touch her, but did not.

'It's our last evening.'

Then she entered the dining-room in the tight black dress which reminded him of her leotard – the high breasts and slender body attracting the attention she craved like a defiant child. And back in their villa the whole charade was washed away. But she answered his lovemaking with a self-obliterating need, her eyes clenched shut, and fell asleep with her fingernails still sharp in his back. For a long time afterwards he lay awake, and at midnight went out onto the verandah to look at the lake. But it was invisible in haze.

When he returned he stood watching her in the faint light, as if in sleep she might divulge some clue to herself. She lay on her side. From her rather small face the hair

66

streamed back over the pillows, and her right arm was extended in front of her as if hunting for him (or someone) on the other side of the bed. Sleep had withdrawn her into herself. She breathed heavily. And as she lay there, her mouth's curves faintly smiling, she seemed in her privacy to be integrated at last – this harlequin woman who maddened and touched and puzzled him – as if all the disparate threads of her had been drawn together by sleep, and no longer needed explanation.

9

The latent disquiet which had trickled through the town began to spread out in a miasma of rumour and fear. The insidious advance of the disease – and it became 'common knowledge' that it was bred by the savages – spilt into Rayner's clinic in a spate of false alarms. Along with the genuine cases – a bank clerk and an eleven-year-old girl – his workload was doubled by healthy people who complained of malaise or eye-ache, or imagined that their skin moles had changed texture and were spreading.

Rumours grew that the savages were infiltrating the town at night, and were exacerbated by the murder of a man in an alley just off the mall. The multiple injuries to his head had been inflicted by axe-blows, and he was half stripped. There were whispers of other murders which the authorities had covered up to forestall panic.

Rayner's apprehension at the natives descended on him again. But one night, too, he woke up from a nightmare of white killers flowering all over the town, as people deflected suspicion by murdering one another with axes. Outside his windows he could see the natives' fires still burning along the river, but the police had stepped up their patrols, and often moved in threes along the bank now, flashlights in hand, while their ghostly launch cruised behind.

Fewer people went out at night. On the outskirts, thick padlocks hung from the compound gates, and more dogs than before had been released into the arid gardens. By day the signs of unease were growing. The public benches and doorways were still scattered with natives, but outside private offices and shops the warning notices multiplied: 'No waiting on steps', 'No lingering'. From time to time, as if to show that something was being done, one of the younger savages would be arrested in the street and taken off for questioning.

Remembering what the old native had said, Rayner prayed only that the rains would come and fill up the water-holes. But every morning revealed the same sultry sky. It seemed to wrap the earth in gauze. Even the birds which flew in it looked suffocated. Rayner, whose foot injury had barred him from military conscription, was liable instead to emergency secondment in the medical corps, and several times found himself attached to jeep patrols among the outlying farms. He saw nothing but sere grass and haggard cattle. Most of the water-holes had been sucked dry, and even the streams shrivelled. The only savages he glimpsed were stick-figures on the horizon, grazing their bullocks in the thorns.

Soon afterwards the garrison commander, a taciturn major, invited him for a drink. He accepted half-heartedly. The infantry company was a patchy unit, whose soldiers had occasionally been jailed for brawling. He found himself in an ambience of bored masculinity, at once harsh and puerile. A few officers were downing beer or whisky in the major's married quarters. Ivar was not among them, and the only women – a pair of sad-faced wives – soon disappeared. Rayner knew that he had not been invited casually, and he was not surprised when a shifty-faced lieutenant of Intelligence prevented him from leaving.

'The commander has a favour to ask,' he said. 'In a way it's a formality.'

As the other guests left, the major opened a door and beckoned Rayner into a spare bedroom. The lieutenant followed, saying, 'Captain Gencer assured us we could count on your discretion.'

Rayner disliked being compromised by Ivar this way. The

bedroom was bare except for basic furniture. As they entered, a small, sallow-skinned man, whom Rayner recognised as the company's medical officer, jumped to his feet and half saluted. How long he had been sitting there was a mystery.

The lieutenant began with absurd delicacy. 'The commander has a *condition*.'

Rayner suddenly knew what was coming. The army doctor was picking tensely at his lapels. The major sat down on the bed and started unbuttoning his jacket. One of the buttons pattered onto the floor.

'The commander . . .' The lieutenant went on speaking for him as if the major were some god or mute. The subaltern's mouth did not seem to belong to the owner of his cold eyes. It enunciated nervously under a thin, charred-looking moustache. 'The commander wishes to know if it is similar to the disease which is spreading in the town.'

The major was lying on the bed now, stripped to the waist, and watched Rayner through watery eyes. In his big, almost hairless head all the features looked incidental, like flaws in stone. It was a strong face, but tired.

'I've given the commander a check-up,' the army surgeon said. 'But we've had no experience in the army with this . . . epidemic.' He looked abject, as if he were personally responsible for the major's disease.

But Rayner, leaning over the patient, saw at once. Down from his left collar-bone and delicately circling the nipple, the rash curled in a malignant-looking river to the base of the ribcage. It followed the same route as it had in the eleven-year-old girl, but whereas it had lain on her skin with a shocking clarity, on the forty-eight-year-old major's it moved across a blemished patchwork of hair and fat-lines and freckles.

Rayner examined the man's eyeballs, the insides of his mouth, but knew the answer already: nothing. The major's stare never left him.

70

The lieutenant said, 'The commander wonders if the rash is similar?'

'Yes, identical.'

The major spoke for the first time. His voice, for so big a man, came small and tense. 'What *is* this disease, doctor?' And Rayner, looking at his eyes and sucked-in lips, recognised the sound for what it was: the fear of death.

He said, 'The truth is, major, we don't know.' But he saw in the man beneath him – in his practical, unreflecting face – a kind of resentment. Whatever the propaganda about his key military post, he was a man in his late forties occupying a dead-end job in a provincial town, and Rayner thought he could hear anger inside that stone carapace of a head. Was this all there was to be?

He felt sorry for him. 'As far as we can tell, the infection limits itself.' He tapped the major's chest. 'Initially the skin pigment changes, but then it stops. There's no development. And the blood shows nothing. At the moment the municipality is trying to trace a common source of infection. In these near-drought conditions, the obvious culprit is the water supply. Tests here haven't yielded results, but samples have been sent up to the state laboratories in the capital, and we're awaiting a verdict.'

As he was speaking the major repeated, '. . . limited infection . . . no development . . . samples to the capital . . .' Rayner wondered how stupid he was. The major grabbed at the information as it flew by, then docketed it away, shorn of complexities.

Rayner asked: 'Is there anything you can help me with? Anything unusual you might have shared with other people recently? Food, perhaps, or anything new?'

The major slowly shook his head. 'Only the air coolers.'

'Air coolers?'

The lieutenant said, 'They're a new invention, doctor. They keep premises cool by some method . . . changing the air. They're better than fans.'

The major sat up and ran his hands cautiously over his chest. 'We're the first to get them. In the barracks.'

So they offered no solution. Rayner asked the major, 'Is there anywhere perhaps you've been?'

The lieutenant tensed. 'I don't think that's a proper question, doctor.'

The major had revived now and was pulling on his jacket. 'What do you mean?' He looked angry.

Rayner burst into laughter. 'Good god, I didn't mean to imply . . .!' His embarrassment detonated round the room. 'No! Hahaha! I know there's a lot of gossip in town about . . . hahah . . . but this disease can't be sexually transmitted . . .' He clapped him on the shoulder. 'You can go anywhere you like, major!'

A phantom smile came to the major's lips. He said, 'Those women . . . they're not my sort, doctor,' then he too started to laugh in a deep, gusty release of nerves, and the room relaxed. The lieutenant's soft mouth snickered, while his eyes watched. Rayner went on chortling. Even the surgeon coughed into the palm of one hand.

In this jittery bloom of laughter the major got to his feet restored. 'Thank you.' He buttoned his jacket firmly, walked to the front door and clasped their hands. It was as if laughter had cleansed away not only their mutual tensions, but the whole native threat, and the epidemic itself. Yet Rayner had simply confirmed what the major had feared, that this was 'the savage plague'. For the moment, it was in abeyance. But what it would become, he could not assess. Perhaps it would remain as it was, an enigmatic mark, whose slight, accompanying malaise would fade away.

As they left, the lieutenant said, 'You understand the need for secrecy on this, doctor?'

'Patients' complaints are always confidential.'

The subaltern went silent, then said, 'But this is exceptional. If it became known, it would destroy confidence.'

Rayner said irritably, 'Perhaps.' In fact he felt that if the major were publicly to admit to the disease, it would lessen its stigma. He curtly said goodnight. He had a sense that the lieutenant was trying to coerce him in some way, to occupy his conscience, and he felt vaguely contaminated. Because the lieutenant insisted on it, the silence he would keep no longer seemed quite moral.

10

They went round and round. Outside the window of their airborne car the funfair lights and the lights of the city streamed together. They huddled inwards, as if at the vortex of a whirlpool, clasping hands. Their knees touched. Because his father was laughing, Rayner imagined that this was his earliest memory; he could not remember his father laughing afterwards. But he was sure of the sound even now – it was guttural, like his own – and the three pairs of linked hands were vivid in his mind. Beyond the lace cuffs fashionable then, the sheen of his mother's fingernails covered his palm, and he recalled the black hairs dusting the back of his father's fist as it enclosed his, and thinking about the mystery of being adult. Probably they circled no more than two metres up in the air, but to him they were spinning into night. A trinity of hands.

'How fast are we going? A *hundred* kilometres!' And he heard his scream of excitement, because it was dangerous, and he was safe.

The analyst asked, 'Your father wasn't a happy man?'

Rayner, surprised by his own answer, said, 'I don't know.' If only he had lived a few years longer – But he'd died with his enigma intact. 'I think he was happy in his work. He was a dour man. Twenty years older than my mother. He always seemed very assured. I expect he calmed my mother just by being himself. I remember our home as very placid, yes, happy, I think . . .'

The man asked, 'You had other relatives?'

'Only one. My father's sister.'

But the house had not been empty, exactly. It had seemed to be visited by people half sketched-in. It was irritating how dimmed they were: family friends, honorary relatives. Nobody important. Except perhaps 'Uncle' Bernard. And even him Rayner remembered as a shadowy *habitué* rather than a distinct presence. He looked a little like his father but kindlier, weaker; and Rayner recalled the gifts he gave more clearly than the man himself: a wooden engine and four carriages with a guard at the back waving a flag; a clockwork acrobat who sprang from his feet to his hands like a jumping bean, until one day he stayed bent double.

'Poor fellow,' said Uncle Bernard. 'I think he's dead.'

Then, to console him, Bernard showed Rayner conjuring tricks. Perhaps that was his job, the boy thought, he seemed to have no other. Sometimes he spent whole afternoons at their house.

'Look! Do you see this penknife? Watch *carefully*. Now where's it gone? . . . You're sure? . . . No, here!'

For that hour he transfigured himself into a wizard. He poured rice out of empty bowls and described the card which the boy held hidden in his hand. But it was the handkerchiefs which Rayner remembered most distinctly. Did the boy know asked Uncle Bernard, that his mother was haunted by beautiful colours? He pulled back the sleeves theatrically from his thin hands. Rayner's mother was sitting between them in a summer dress. She was always animated when Bernard came, and now she was laughing in advance.

'There! . . . There! . . . and there!' He plucked them from her ears, from her hair, from the nape of her neck: brilliant-coloured satin kerchiefs which dropped in the boy's lap. It was mesmerising. Rayner could scarcely track the fingers flashing back and forth. Nor could his mother. Her hands followed Bernard's, trying to stop him, but her laughter bubbled up as if she were being tickled. She looked beautiful, he thought.

Even Bernard seemed carried away. 'And there's one

scarf left. The blue one! Where does she keep the blue one?'

Then, out of the gentle cleft between her breasts, he pulled a stream of silk turquoise. 'There!'

The boy simply gazed. He could not understand. Suddenly his mother seemed awesome to him, different. Bernard might be a wizard, but the repository of magic, of all these secret colours, was she. Why was Bernard the only one who knew that she carried this beauty with her? Had she not told his father? He fingered the satins on his knees. They seemed real. Even the turquoise one; but how did Bernard know she kept it there?

Long afterwards he wondered how deeply Uncle Bernard had dipped his fingers into his mother's cleft, but he could not be sure. And now Bernard was asking, 'Will you be a conjuror when you grow up?'

But Rayner was already stubborn. It was a private vow with him to be a lawyer. He whispered this out.

'So he wants to follow his papa!' There was a glint of mockery in the voice. 'Is he more like his papa or his mama?' Bernard's face came circling round Rayner's. 'I think you should follow your mother. She's a conjuror too, you know!' He took her hand, lifted it into the air, and as if from her fingertips there bloomed a silver cigarette case. 'I think he's more like his mother!'

'That's enough, Bernard,' she said.

In Rayner's memory the wonder and oddness of all this held a tinge of distress. He felt he was being moved against his father, against his will. He decided he did not like Uncle Bernard any more. In those days his family could still afford a nurse, and he was glad, for once, when she was summoned to take him for a walk.

Rayner said: 'It was just harmless fun, of course. And soon afterwards Uncle Bernard faded out.'

'Faded out?'

'Yes, people did that in my parents' world.' It was the

76

analyst's silence which irritated him, Rayner thought. The man just sat there. 'In any case, I realise now that my mother was not an attractive woman.'

The analyst joked for the first time. 'That's always a matter of opinion!'

'And after my father's death she simply caved in. She didn't seem to have anything left. She started drinking. It was pathetic, I know, but a sign of her love.'

The man did not answer. His pen dangled over his notepad. He did not direct Rayner, did not suggest explanations, in fact never said anything definite at all. If he were not the only doctor practising therapy in the town – psychoanalysis was such a young science here – Rayner would have gone elsewhere. 'You may want a trauma from my childhood,' he said, 'but I'm hard put to find you one. The nearest thing was a fire. When I was five we had a fire outbreak in the house one night. My father was away on business and my mother had to rescue me. I was dreaming I was on a railway station, but there was real smoke in my nostrils.'

He was woken by his own coughing and by a woman howling somewhere. It was pitch dark, but he felt a new presence in the room: thick and pungent. He reached for his bedside lamp and as he switched it on the door flew open. The whole room seemed to be hung with gauze, and on the far side, a long way away, she was standing with her hands at her throat. She appeared as if she had already been through flames. Her hair hung wild, her clothes crumpled and her face and hands looked stained with soot. He began to cry. Then she came towards him, as if parting the gauze, and held out her arms. Her voice was husky with smoke. 'Come to me.'

The analyst was watching him. 'So your mother rescued you.'

'Yes. I can't remember what happened after that . . . We never spoke about it in the family afterwards.'

'Why not?'

77

'I don't know . . . I can't remember.'

But his memory was like that; it splintered even recent events. Sometimes he could remember nothing of an encounter except a vivid, trivial detail. The whole heart and importance of the episode would have disappeared, leaving behind the nicotine on a man's fingernails or the colour of a child's eyelashes. Only in remembering his absent friends did the details synthesise into full portraits, as though their minutiae had overlaid and reinforced one another. So Leon, with his delicate lips and rounded paleness, and fine-boned Jarmila in her fair waterfall of hair, assembled easily in his mind.

And, of course, Miriam.

The analyst, who normally let him ramble, asked, 'What was so distinctive about this girl?'

'She was very warm,' Rayner said at once. 'It was expressed in her body. She was brown, vital.' His hands unfurled from his chest. 'She had this special gift for drawing out . . . I can't exactly explain.'

'First love.' The doctor's gaze was fixed on the wall beside him. 'Very potent.'

'Yes, and the place was right,' Rayner said forcefully. 'I was brought up there. She belonged to that world. It was natural to us.' He did not know where the man's home town was, but he added austerely, 'I think it's simply better than anywhere else.'

The analyst did not answer.

Rayner wished he could articulate precisely what he felt, but he only said, 'I think you belong with your past,' and the words, as he spoke them, became true. He was thinking, curiously, of the church at the end of their street in the capital, the whitewashed and pinnacled sanctuary in whose graveyard his parents were buried. Whether or not you believed (and Rayner did not), the building seemed to hold in focus all the social unity, the flow of past into future which he had lost. He knew it by heart: the plaster Virgin

78

in her field of tapers; the Christus Victor on the altar; the memorial plaques to soldiers and priests (and even a state councillor): 'Revered Memory . . . *Prudens et Fidelis* – the bones of . . . *Vitae Morumque Exemplar . . .*' it was the church of Miriam, Leon and Adelina. They'd been confessed and confirmed there as a row of giggling children. There he had lost his faith insidiously, without pain. But now that he was exiled in this pragmatic, near-atheist town, he realised that his childhood church had gathered up its citizens – dark-clothed and formal – and pointed them in a direction which had nothing to do with the town's pragmatism. It looked out onto otherness, mystery.

'Everybody was there.' Miriam glowed by his hospital bedside. 'Even the side chapels were full.'

Rayner, dazed by concussion and chloroform, only now understood that she was talking about his mother's funeral. She bent down and kissed him. He said, 'What about the autopsy?'

'Oh, that was clear. Were you worried?'

'You knew her, poor mama. I hope nobody detected . . . alcohol.'

'Good heavens, no!' Suddenly her hands were caressing his cheeks. He was too weak to touch her. He simply stared. Her brimming body belonged so extravagantly to the wondrous species of the healthy. Her face came smiling high above his. She said, 'She was cleared of all blame. How good to be the first to tell you!' Her fingers started a teasing tattoo along his plastered leg. 'You were hit by one of those armoured state postal vans. Their drivers are all mad.'

Rayner was to realise only by degrees that his mother was dead. Now he felt that by surviving, he had abandoned her. And there had been no goodbye. He tried to smile at Miriam. If only he could have gone to the funeral, he felt, that would have been a kind of farewell.

'It was right you didn't go.' She lifted her chin. 'It would have been cruel. Why put yourself through that? It's better to remember happiness. Actually, I *hate* funerals. I think they're morbid and pointless. It's better to look back on the good things.'

Three times afterwards Rayner had returned to the church and sat at the rear of the empty nave, looking towards the altar. Like that, it reimposed its mystique, and there was room for God in it.

The church had awed him since childhood. Once, as a boy of ten, he had wandered in alone. He had never seen it empty before, and became afraid of the tap of his feet on the tiles. The tapers under the Virgin had gone out. But the stained-glass saints glared at him from their sun, and the memorial plaques were dripping plaster veils and fear. He tiptoed into the chancel. From their corbels he was being watched by painted angels' faces, with headbands and girlish hair. On the altar's golden crucifix the eyes of the hanging Christ blazed out under a crown of thorns and glory. They did not see him.

On an impulse Rayner took out of his pocket the crystal given him by a scrawny waif called Anna. It was scarcely bigger than a marble, but when you shook it the glass filled with snowflakes. This mystery (he had never seen snow) and his wonder at the girl, turned it unique. Gingerly he placed it at the foot of the implacable-looking Christ, and backed away. He might have meant it as an offering or a claim for Anna: a stake in holiness. He was not sure.

Next Sunday, at mass, he saw it still on the altar – a secret blasphemy – and nobody noticing. But he looked at it with despair. During the intervening days it seemed to have been sucked away from him into the aura of the crucifix. He had planned to recover it, full of manna from its adventure. But he did not dare. It was infected too deeply with the magic of the chancel, through lying hour after hour under the nailed and golden feet, bathed in the stained-glass cross-fire of the saints. It had withdrawn from him. Yet for all he knew the pang of loss he felt was for the girl, who was not in church that morning, so that the crystal seemed to have returned into God, and she with it, leaving him on the far side.

11

As the disease spread, and the rains did not come, the town simmered in suspension. A surface normality reigned, but a new energy went into preserving it. Even in the streets people walked with a look of responsibiliy, as if embattled, and their talk was edgy. Tiny distress signals multiplied. A few weeks earlier, anything thought indigenous to the land – from banana fibre to sweet potatoes – had shown a price tag stamped with a smiling native. These had now vanished; and the shops which once displayed native-woven mats and baskets were selling other things.

Everybody knew that the situation had outstripped the police, and that decisions now rested with the army. Their jeep patrols rumbled out into the country every morning, scouring the stock-breeding lands at the foot of the mountains, and sometimes at sunset, if you saw them return, you would glimpse the blank face of a captured savage among the soldiery. There were random arrests at night, usually in the dry river beds along the town's outskirts. But almost nobody witnessed them. And nobody asked if the natives were returned. After a rumour that their dogs were spreading the disease, all strays were shot on sight. Yet there was no official curfew, and every morning people would wake to a new swathe of graffiti blazoned across public buildings. The latest of them, inscribed on the walls of the telephone exchange, simply said: 'Kill them'.

Rayner spent more time than usual operating the erratic radiotelegraph which connected his clinic with outlying cattle stations. Many farming people only needed reassurance, but he could not truthfully give it. Their women came in pregnant from the stations now at thirty-five weeks, begging for beds. He never got away from work before dusk.

After a week of such days he emerged from his clinic to find an army staff car waiting for him. Its driver said, 'There's a job for you up at barracks, sir.' He hated being at the military's disposal, but Leszek was too old and nervous to go. So he climbed into the car, with a vague foreboding.

In the twilight the town was closing itself down. They left behind the expensive stucco villas with their flimsy wrought-iron and frangipani trees, and entered a poorer district. People had already abandoned the streets. Through the slats of their shanties, lifted on concrete stilts above the termites, faint lamplight showed or jazz drifted. Their tin roofs were rusting to shreds, and the gardens rampaged with dogs. The sun set in a torrid blur, as it had for weeks. To Rayner, feverish with humidity, it seemed that only the rain could restore this place, and cleanse the air of fear.

Instead of a lounging duty guard, two armed sentries monitored them at the gates. They drove on under search-lights across a tarmac parade ground, where twelve-pound field guns flanked an empty flagstaff, then on through a military police compound, and stopped outside the army surgeon's door. The driver said, 'It's through there.'

At that moment the door swung open and Ivar came out. 'Rayner! I didn't want to trouble you' – he squeezed his hand – 'but one of the prisoners needs medical attention. You'll understand when you see him.' Ivar looked suavely regretful, as if he had caused some embarrassment. 'I have to go, but the lieutenant will advise you.'

So Rayner went in alone. The room was stifling. It was more like a prison cell than a surgery. A white-draped bed under a powerful overhead lamp did service as an operating table, and the medicine shelves showed lines of yellowing labels and discoloured lints. The prisoner was sitting in a chair facing the Intelligence lieutenant, while between them stood a stout corporal, one of the half-breed natives whom the army used as trackers and interpreters.

'The prisoner fell during a fight with another inmate,' the lieutenant said. 'I don't think it's too serious.'

Rayner stooped to examine the man. He was a young savage with a flat, brutal face. His eyes were charcoal slits. Down from his left eyebrow ploughed a jagged, three-inch gash. Its blood still soaked his shirt.

Rayner asked casually, 'Where did you collect this man?'

'He was hanging around one of the farms upriver. He had a gun. We took him in as a precaution.' The lieutenant's voice fluted and cooed. 'Then he lost his head.'

Rayner straightened and said, 'I'll need ether for this.'

'You've handled this size of wound before, haven't you?'

'Yes, but not under these conditions.' He hunted the surgeon's shelves, but there were no ether masks, not even chloroform, and half the bottles were empty or unlabelled.

'What's wrong with just sterilising it?' The lieutenant's voice tinkled on his girl's lips. But his eyes were saying: *It's only a savage. They don't feel anything.*

'It'll need extra care.' Rayner thought: Perhaps it's surer, the man may be more frightened of ether than of the needle. He asked the interpreter, 'Tell him to lie on the bed. Tell him that I'm a doctor and that I'm going to sew his skin together again.'

The interpreter took the savage's arm and guided him to the operating table. His native speech sounded crazed to unaccustomed ears. It lurched between bunched consonants and a hoarse torrent of phonemes. He seemed to be abusing the prisoner, but no expression arrived on either of their faces. The man might have heard nothing at all. But he followed the corporal's arm to the bed, and lay down. His hair bushed round his head like a pillow.

Rayner asked, 'Does he understand you? Are you from the same clan?'

84

The intrepreter said, 'He's from the Ningumiri. But he understands me all right. He's just not meeting us.'

When Rayner started cleaning the wound, the prisoner did not stir, only stared up at the lamp. It was the face of a pitiless statue. The only signs of its unease were the vertical ridges which lifted faintly in the centre of the forehead. But in this brighter light Rayner could see that the skin around the wound was minutely, evenly serrated, as if it had been sawed. He asked, 'What actually caused this?'

The lieutenant said, 'He fell.'

'But what hit him? What did it? This isn't compatible with a fall.'

'I don't know. I wasn't there.' The lieutenant's tone had tightened. 'Is it relevant?'

'Yes it is.' Rayner felt a prick of anger. 'If I knew the answer I'd be able to assess the chances of infection.' He turned to the interpreter. 'Ask the prisoner what caused this.'

The interpreter's eyes flicked to the lieutenant, and back. Then he turned to the native and resumed his bursts of vowels and glottal consonants. Rayner was aware that he might have been saying anything, and that neither he nor the lieutenant would know. Perhaps, Rayner imagined, the corporal's own savage heritage was more potent than his white blood, and he was saying: 'Stay silent. These whites are all bastards.' Or maybe his army uniform obliterated any racial fellow-feeling: 'If you answer the doctor's question, we'll beat the hell out of you.'

Whatever he said, no reply came. The savage went on staring at the ceiling as if he were deaf. Yet somewhere behind those sunk eyes, Rayner sensed, the man understood. It was apparent in the set of his full, belligerent mouth.

Rayner leant over him and tried to see into his eyes. He demanded, 'Tell me, what hit you?'

The lieutenant stirred behind him. But the savage never moved. The corporal, for some reason, was smiling.

Rayner mistrusted the surgeon's implements, and used his own. As he dipped his needle into the half-numbed skin, he did not know what the native's reaction would be. But again there was none. Rayner might as well have been stitching the man's clothes. Only when he adjusted the overhead lamp, lowering it closer to the bed, the ridges on the native's forehead trembled with sudden fear and his eyes opened to show bloodshot whites. But the moment Rayner resumed his stitching, drawing the skin over the raw wound, the man's face resettled into its black halo of hair, and seemed at peace.

The sweat started trickling from Rayner's forehead into his eyes. By the time he had finished, he felt unnaturally exhausted. He packed his implements back into his case without a word.

The lieutenant said, 'We know we can count on your discretion.'

Rayner snapped, 'You're lucky you can.' But he realised that the statement was meaningless. Nobody in the town would care what happened in this prison, and some would feel a secret pleasure. He wiped the sweat from his lips and touched the prisoner's shoulder, uncomprehended.

'Rest now.'

The same staff car was waiting outside to drive him back. The streets were deserted. Their few lamps spread dangerous pools of light in the dark. The whole town had gone silent, locked in its private dreams and nightmares. A three-quarter moon hung overhead, and a few of the desert deer had strayed in and were grazing on the verges.

Rayner must have let out an involuntary groan, because the driver turned round and said, 'Are you all right, sir?'

'Yes,' he said. 'I'm all right.'

The sweat had dried on his forehead, and even his anger had ebbed. But he pulled the towel from his case and wiped his hands, his neck, his lips, over and over. He just wanted to get out of here.

12

Rayner's villa had subtly transformed. During the seven years he had lived there, it had continued to look bare, cool and too big for him, as if briefly rented. It resembled, in fact, the place of transition he believed it to be.

But Zoë vitalised it. She came and went between the villa and her flat, borrowing his books and bringing back textiles or rugs which she hung on the offending blank walls. He enjoyed the way she moved so easily in and out. They seemed to have an unspoken treaty not to coerce one another. Sometimes she would stay for a few hours, sometimes for several days. He never knew. But where previous girlfriends had tried to feminise the villa, suggesting prettier curtain designs or buying him vases and ornaments, Zoë left behind a bright, personal trail of things she had forgotten or wanted him to keep, and spread a kind of zany Bohemia. It was oddly uninvasive. She would appropriate a wall or an alcove, impatient with its starkness, then forget whatever she had put there – a copper bowl, a flowering shrub, a stuffed armadillo – and sometimes replace it later as if it had been his. At other times she would discover mementoes and photographs which he had stowed away in the louvred cupboards, and would impudently set them up on view. 'There! Why do you hide your past from me?' And he would find himself living with his parents again in the inaccessible capital.

Little by little, to his secret pleasure, her possessions intermingled with his. Her novels and yoga manuals became incorporated among his medical texts, histories and travel books, and his classical records were infiltrated by jazz. In the bedroom cupboards her summer dresses came to hang among his drab jackets, and a flotilla of small shoes appeared; and when he hunted the bathroom shelves for razor blades he found her setting-pins and tweezers instead.

Usually she brought her cat with her: the only guarantee of an overnight stay. It was mercurial, independent and a little fierce, like her. Its variegated coat, he told her, was a symbol of her personality, and depending on her mood he would lift the creature up in front of her and point to an area of fur – black, brindled, white or furious orange. He had come to sense when she wanted to be alone by the preoccupied way she moved about; then he would simply lift up the cat, point to black fur and disappear into his study or the garden. Her moods, he sensed, were a part of her self-reassurance. They were saying, 'I do not belong to him.' They made him perversely sad. He loved her independence; but it unnerved him.

Their working hours were at odds. In the morning, after finishing her dance exercises, Zoë went out to teach yoga to bored businessmen's wives, who averted their collective gaze from what she did in the evening, but who all wanted to look like her. At dusk, just as he returned, she would be gone, and he would enter rooms in which the musty odour of his own solitude had been replaced by the smells of her day: nail varnish, vegetarian cooking, cat food, and the sweetish scent of her sweat after exercise. And on the bed two or three of her costumes would lie discarded in a shimmering pile of lamé, aigrette and batwing sleeves.

On one of these evenings he returned to a letter from his aunt in the capital. The writing on the envelope had become a tremulous mockery of its old self, but the message inside retained the austere factuality of his father's sister. 'My health has declined,' she wrote, 'and I am arranging for the eventual disposal of this house. As you are my closest surviving relative, it will pass to you, and I will inform you when the lawyers need your attendance. Your temporary residence permit here can be arranged.'

He tried to imagine her. Even fifteen years ago, when he'd last seen her, she had looked formidably old. After his father's death she had continued to come to lunch on most Sundays – to his mother's distress – wearing a brown bombazine dress, long out of fashion. A quaint toque hat generally roosted on her head, he remembered, but this was the only ridiculous thing about Aunt Birgit. The moment she removed it, you were confronted by a face of white, aquiline power.

Rayner's sudden elation had nothing to do with the money. It was the prospect of the capital which filled him with impatience.

'Who is this aunt?' Zoë asked.

'She's my father's younger sister. She never married. But everything I heard about her came from my parents, and that wasn't much. So when you ask who she is, I realise I don't know. As a boy I was a bit in awe of her.' His childhood had been full of people like that, he remembered: people of whom 'Who is she?' died on the lips. 'I could never picture her young.'

Zoë listened. Rayner intrigued her when he tried to imagine people's lives, because that was not the sort of imagining she could do. She embraced or rejected people on instinct.

'I think my aunt must be dying. She owned this house on the same street as ours. It's valuable.' But when he thought about how little it interested him, he felt distantly sad for her: this old woman, who would die out there on the fringes of his memory, leaving nothing to anybody loved. All at once he asked Zoë, 'Do you need money?'

'No!' She laughed, suddenly tender. 'What would I need money for?'

'Cat food?' How strange, he thought. Money could do so little for either of them. The recognition of this must separate them from almost anybody else in the town. 'My aunt must have more influence than I thought,' he said. 'She says she can get me a two-week residence permit.'

'It'd be good for you to go back. You'll see your old friends.' But Zoë said this gravely, as if after long silence, touching his chest with her fingertips, and he realised that the idea unnerved her. 'You'll see the sea.' He sensed her apprehension. He was going away to the city most natural to him, from which she had been banished. She took up the letter to reread it, then tossed it back onto the table. 'You'll pick up old threads.' But she could not keep still, as if the carpet were shifting under her feet.

Rayner felt a warm, selfish relief at these symptoms of her love, her dependence. But a growing wretchedness too. Because he knew that one day he would go back for good. He said, 'Do you have any family or contacts left there?'

'No.'

'I wonder how much things have changed.' He began to sound falsely jocular, because he felt guilty. 'There might be new job openings for you, something you could get a residence permit for.' But the moment he said this he realised it was fantasy. Who ever went up to the capital from a provincial cabaret? Yet guilt and sadness drove him on: guilt that it would be this city – perhaps soon – which would separate them. He did not want to think about it. He wanted to believe that she would be there too. 'I could look around for you.'

But Zoë was suddenly angry. All the lines of her face converged on her eyes. 'Why the hell should I go back there? What's the point? They killed off their floor shows years ago. There's nothing left but puppets and ballroom dancing!'

He said, 'You've kept so fit, you could go back into ballet.'

'Ballet!' She spat out the word. Why should I go back

into the ballet? I left the capital to get away from all that. Christ. Dying swans and Sleeping Beauties! I just don't *feel* like that. I'm not a swan, and I'm not beautiful.' She washed a hand across her face as if wiping off its mask. 'At least the dancing here is true. It's *mine*. Why should I dance falsely there when I can dance properly here?'

'For one thing, you'd get a better kind of spectator . . .' Rayner was starting to hate himself. But he could not believe that in her heart she did not want to return.

'God damn the spectators!' She glared at him. 'I'll dance just for *myself* if I have to. At least that'd be better than pretending!' She stared down at her feet. 'I couldn't go back to that bloody ballet. I haven't done an *entrechat* in ten years. Anyway, how do you know a theatre audience is any better? Those posh people. They're probably wanking in their pants just like in the night club.' Once, in a priggish moment, Rayner had attributed her swearing, when she became excited, to 'the coarseness of her profession'. She had not forgiven this. 'Yes, I know what you're thinking, they'd *never* talk like that in the capital.'

'*You* were born near the capital. You should know.'

'I don't give a fuck for the capital. I'm *here*. *Now*. And that's okay with me, except that you're . . . you're . . .' She faltered. She made as if to face him, but did not, and he saw that her cheeks were shining with tears. '. . . Except that you're obsessed with going back.'

Then she thrust back her shoulders, uncaring of her face for once, which was bleeding mascara and tears, and faced him squarely. 'How long have we been lovers? Three months now. And you haven't understood a thing.'

But they both knew that beneath his speciousness he was saying: *I mean to return to the capital for good. I wish you could come too.*

And that she was answering: *You know I can't.*

She went off into another room, slamming the door behind her. Rayner stayed where he was, kicking at the table leg, too proud to follow and apologise. Sometimes, he thought, Zoë appeared to have lost hope, and was just angrily resigned to where and who she was; but at other times, as now, she simply seemed realistic, and made him feel a child.

He pushed open the door. She was perched on the kitchen table, inspecting the cat. She had let her hair down in an act of unconcern. The cat's claws were tangled in it. The mascara had dried on her cheeks.

She looked up and said at once, 'How can I explain to you? I'm not happy with what I'm doing, but it's the best I have to go on with. If I could, I'd make the world different, but I can't. So I dance my kind of dance in the only place that will accept me.' She detached the cat's claws. 'I'm sorry it's not the state opera house.'

He felt too ashamed to touch her. He went to the sink and started washing glasses which she had already washed. 'You pour so much energy into your work . . . It just annoys me that it's only for those . . . They're only hoping you'll strip . . .' He ended lamely, 'You know I admire your dancing.'

But when he watched her dance now he did not know whether he was admiring it through her, or loving her through it. Sometimes, unpredictably, she would arrive home glowing with the applause she had received: generally from the middle-aged people who came early in the evening. Then the depth of her pleasure moved him, and he would be astonished again at this violent, hopeless quest for recognition in such a place, and at her refusal to become what it wanted her to be.

She said more softly, 'I don't see the differences in people like you do. You always see the differences. But even the men in that club aren't all bad, and maybe something I do gets home to one or two of them, and they think *that's dancing*, instead of what they're usually thinking.'

Rayner took her head in his hands, not knowing if she

would wrench it away, but she only looked down. When he picked the cat out of her lap and pointed to its furious orange fur, a wavering smile started on her mouth, then disappeared.

Suddenly he said, '*I'm sorry*,' and the words sounded intense, broken. Sorry, they were saying, not only for his misconceived wishes for her, but for his own divisive hopes, which were for himself. Yet he felt that he did love her, in his fractured and limited way, quite violently.

She said, 'I'm not ashamed of what I do.'

'I know. That shows.' She carried a kind of flawed pride with her, and this self-image seemed to establish her literal worth. But the ambience in which it played itself out was endlessly confusing to him, as if the strippers, the dimmed lights, the prurient audience painted over her a thin, contaminating varnish.

Yet he was erotically proud of the dancer on the little stage. He loved her body in motion. Even at home, when she dressed or undressed, he would watch the lift of her soft arms and tight breasts, the flicker of her calves. And when she emerged into the club's spotlight, slimmer and more vivid than her daytime self, he would sense the restlessness of other men all round him. 'She'd be a hard lay,' he heard one man mutter. But their anger, if it came, was only frustration, he knew, because her dance was saying: I am like this, but you cannot have me. Then he would realise with wonder that her inaccessible beauty would lie beside him tonight.

Loving her, he told her playfully, was like enjoying illusion and reality together.

'But I don't dance an illusion,' she said crossly. 'I'm the only one who doesn't.'

'Perhaps you only imagine you're dancing your real self,' he teased her. 'All that going into battle. All that apparent confidence. Showing off your body.'

'That's too clever,' she said.

But the important thing was momentarily to believe the illusion, Rayner thought, and there swam into his head a memory of small girls dancing in somebody's hall. They were rigged out in white- and silver-woven tutus and crowns. It was his job to keep the gramophone wound up and playing *The Sleeping Beauty*. Jarmila – blonde, twelve-year-old Jarmila – was the acknowledged ballerina among them (even by Miriam, who was proud) and her conviction carried the day. She performed precocious bourrées and arabesques. Unlike Zoë, she knew that she was beautiful, and a swan. It was a matter of who you imagined you were.

It was late. Zoë put the cat to bed on it cushion. Then she cleansed her face, swearing at its smeared mascara. 'How long have I been looking like that? You must have been laughing at me.'

'I wasn't.'

For a while she lay sexlessly in his arms, withdrawn into one of her darknesses. At such moments, with deepening wretchedness, he felt her imprisoned in a past which he could not enter, back in the shadow of her parents, her merciless lovers, her stillborn child.

He wanted to make love to her, as if this were to give her something. But it might be her gift to him. 'I'm sorry I was such a fool.'

'Don't talk.' Her body turned against his. 'You can tell me I'm beautiful if you like.' That was the sadness in her speaking. 'Otherwise don't talk.'

But he demanded between kisses, 'Why not talk? Do you sometimes try to forget me when we make love?'

But she only frowned. 'Perhaps I've had the wrong sort of men for too long. You're not that sort of man.' She touched his head to her breast. 'Perhaps I can't associate sex with love any more. I don't know.' Yet she seemed unconscious of the pathos in the conjecture. 'I don't know what any of it means.'

13

As Rayner finished his morning clinic and checked the waiting-room, he found Leszek's last patients huddled round the walls with their gaze averted from its centre. There, immobile on their quilt, sat the old savage and his blank-faced daughter. She was wearing the same crumpled white dress, but her father had put on a loose-fitting shirt and bound his grey hair with a headband. They sat there like emanations of the wilderness. Nobody even glanced at them. But as the old man lumbered to his feet, the incongruity of his standing there, so rough-hewn and immobile, seemed to deplete him. His open-air majesty had dropped away. He looked rather helpless.

He said, 'I come because I think something not right when I in that place. You say, if you get to town, come see me.'

Rayner led him into his room, and the girl followed. The other patients' faces lifted in unison to watch them.

The old man sat down on the edge of the examination couch. The girl fidgeted beside him. Her movements were sudden and frightened. And now Rayner saw that her father was changed. He seemed no longer to control the bulk of flesh which enclosed him. His life had shrivelled inside it. Even his expression seemed to have withdrawn into his thicket of beard and locks, leaving little behind but a swarming nose and overcast eyes.

Rayner said: 'What do you feel is wrong?'

The old man flexed his arm, testing it. 'It went wrong back there, in that place, three days ago.' His look of puzzlement, the natives' knotting of nose and brows, seemed suddenly fitting. He gazed at Rayner. 'I wake up with this feeling, like a ghost has been living in me. Yes, like that. Like somebody done something to me in the night while I'm sleeping. But there's nobody been in that place for two days. Just me and my daughter.'

'What did it feel like?'

'Well, I get up thinking: who's been here? Then I bend for my trousers and my fingers don't take them. My arm is somewhere else, it's left me. So I say to my daughter, pick up my trousers. I say that in my head, but my mouth doesn't make words at all. See, I've lost my control. As if my body taken by some other feller. So I pick up the trousers with my other hand, and that's okay. But when I try talk again the words come out wrong, like a baby. Yes, that's how it is, like a baby.'

When Rayner examined him he found, as he expected, that his blood pressure was high; and on its left side the corrugations of his forehead had relaxed unnaturally, and a faint slackness released one corner of his mouth.

'You didn't see yourself in a mirror after this?'

'Mirror?' A guttural laugh rocked the man's shoulders. 'What'd an old man have a mirror for? I given up looking at myself. I done with all that.'

'Did you have trouble eating?'

'The girl says the food come out of my mouth. Yes, I find it in my beard. But not any more. Is okay now.'

'What about your eyes?'

'Eyes, they're hard to shut at first.' He dug his fingers into their lids. 'When we started out to town, everything worse than now. But it gets better with walking.'

'How long were you walking?'

'Two days.'

Rayner thought: then he's still strong, he may carry on for a few years.

The old man settled his look of puzzlement on him, but with an unfocused gaze, as if he descried some figure on a skyline deep in Rayner's skull. 'So what is this thing? Is it one of those that come back?'

'You've had a mild stroke.' Rayner watched the man's face, but it yielded nothing. 'It means you've got to be careful or it could come back.' But he wondered what to advise. The old man's diet was already almost free of salts and animal fats, and in any case, little in his way of living would change now. 'I'll give you some tablets.'

He made up a packet of bromide, but knew that it was little more than a placebo. 'Take one tablet every day. It'll make your body calmer.'

The man took them in his oddly delicate hands, then passed them to his daughter.

Rayner asked, 'You'll remember?'

The old man did not answer. He seemed to have forgotten, or dismissed, the tablets. Instead he flexed his left arm again. 'What about this? Is not like before. My grip still gone a bit.'

'That may get better. Don't stop using it.'

The girl held the bromide in front of her, like a trophy. Her father got to his feet. He quivered faintly all through his frame. When he went to the door his gait was stiffly frail, but Rayner remembered it had been like that before.

'Where will you go now?'

They turned in the doorway, side by side. They resembled a primitive icon, he thought: their faces both unreadable. Like all the savages, they seemed at once contented and melancholy. This was their mystery to him. He repeated, 'Where will you go now? Have you relatives anywhere?'

'Relatives all too far from here, I reckon,' the old man said. 'My father come from Piat country but his people they all left. I not been in that country for long time. That's all Mingala now.'

But to Rayner these names and boundaries were all meaningless. He and the native lived on different maps. To the old man the few towns and linked roads were incidental to the flux and ebb of herdsmen over the grasslands.

Rayner asked, 'Can you come back and see me? Can you get transport from that place?'

'We go somewhere else,' the man said. 'Water not so good in that place. I reckon it won't last.'

'Can you come back here in a few days?'

'We come back.' But the old man said it without conviction, like a formula. Then he turned his back heavily in the doorway and his daughter followed him out, still carrying the tablets in front of her.

Rayner heard them walk through the waiting-room, and into the street. He felt relief at their going – things were difficult enough here as it was – followed by self-disgust. If they'd been townspeople, he thought, he would have kept the man under observation for three or four weeks, checking his blood pressure and the taking of his pills. As it was, father and daughter would disappear back into the wilderness, where he would perhaps die.

Rayner went into the waiting-room, where Leszek's last patient, a balloon-faced woman holding crutches, asked at once, 'Did they have it, doctor?'

He controlled his irritation. 'The disease has no connection with the natives. That's all nonsense. We haven't diagnosed a single case among them.'

All the same, his anxiety had deepened. The epidemic was spreading. Even a long-term prisoner in the town jail had developed it. And the water supply analysis from the state laboratories had supplied no clue.

He walked out into the street. The natives had gone barely fifty metres along the pavement, the father's hand weighing on his daughter's shoulder. Something about their backs as they moved – the weakened stoop of the man, the girl's innocent slenderness – made them unbearably vulnerable. Rayner heard himself sigh with exasperation as he followed them. The girl was carrying a bag and a rolled-up quilt. He called out in a voice still harsh with annoyance, 'If you settle near here I can keep an eye on you. There's a piece of parkland just above the river.'

They turned and stared.

He touched the old man's arm. 'I'll need to check on you during the next three weeks. If you stay above the river, you shouldn't be disturbed. Have you got any food, any money?'

'We got all those things,' the man said. 'We going upriver, but if you want maybe we stay here a little, eh. You show us the place.'

Rayner took them back along the street behind the clinic. Passers-by stared in hostility, and he imagined how they would talk. Mutely he hated the old man for moving so slowly. Then he was ashamed at his own shame, and glowered back at the passers-by, suppressing their stares.

In the scrubland between the clinic and his home grew a copse of bloodwood trees and acacia, concealed from the road and the river. But as he led the natives across it they were all flagrantly exposed, and he knew people must be watching.

Then the copse pulled a screen round them. The girl spread the quilt under a tree and took a wooden mixing-bowl and some medicine-grass out of the bag. Her father sat down, and seemed content. She knelt beside him. Rayner said, 'If you start feeling worse, you get back to the clinic. I'll come and see you some days, to check your blood.'

The man's head turned slowly, levelly, viewing the copse. His far-focused eyes and flared nostrils seemed to be listening to it, Rayner thought, deciding on it. He said, 'This okay, this place. We can stay.'

'You'll stay three weeks?' Rayner crouched beside him.

'Well, maybe. But we need to go back. Back to some place where our people passing through. I thinking about my daughter. She needs marry.' The girl was soaking the medicine grass with a gourd of water. 'But okay we stay here some.'

Rayner wondered where his people were, his clan, his vanished family. The natives seemed to splinter and coalesce mysteriously, almost at random. 'Just don't go into the middle of town too often. Things have got worse between the blacks and whites. A lot of rumours going about.'

'I seen the way people look.'

'And don't camp by the river at night. The army patrols it.'

The old man took off his headband and laid it on the quilt, releasing his hair to circle him like a huge, disordered ruff. 'I seen the army, three trucks out in the bush. Gangs of blackfellers too, got hunting spears in the old way. And some got guns.'

Rayner had heard of these groups: as many as fifteen or twenty men, armed as if for raiding. The soldiers never seemed to find them, but last week they had surprised a native breaking into a house on the outskirts, and had shot him dead. Most of the townspeople had shown open satisfaction at this, imagining that something had at last been done.

Back in the capital, Rayner remembered, people had talked about the sanctity of individual life. But here a human life was a negotiable unit. There were too many poor ones to pretend that they deeply mattered.

'These groups all over the bush,' the old man said. 'Some there, some here. One party come to the ancestor place, where we was. Our people think that if you camp round the ancestors, you get strong.'

'What are these groups doing?'

'They just living, mostly. But some afraid of the soldiers, and maybe some just bad in the head and want to kill whitefeller, and the drought make them silly. Yes, lots of fellers got spears now, just to help themselves, or to make revenge, see. Is everything changed. Everyone talking and

100

getting scared.' But he spoke as if such things were already receding from him in his age and sickness, growing meaningless. 'I reckon this country going back to the old times. I remember when white soldiers and blackfellers shooting all over the bush. But that now sixty years ago, when I a long way very little. I never think I see that again.'

Rayner glanced up at the bald sky. 'Perhaps the rains will come.'

But the old man said, 'I reckon the sky dried out now. Is too late for rains. We had one year like this when I was a boy. Water-holes emptied, and dead cattle all over the bush. Some fellers went mad, started killing.' His breathing had grown heavy again. 'I reckon we got that kind of year.'

Rayner stood up. The girl had already mulched the grass and was pouring its liquid back into the gourd. She did not seem to notice when he said goodbye, but her father gazed up at him with an expression which might have been gratitude, and lifted his hand in a half-salute. Looking back from the copse's edge, Rayner saw them seated side by side as if on silent picnic, embalmed in the noon glare, motionless. Above them the sky and the bloodwood trees were drained of colour. The two natives could have been at prayer. They reminded Rayner of the painted scarp of their own ancestors, whose faded figures seemed to inhabit some primitive Eden.

14

The town's fear was heightened by a sense that the wilderness was closing in on it. By August a haze of bush fires hovered across every horizon, and blurred the circle of the sun. The savages, it was said, were systematically setting fire to the scrublands, and the tinder-dry shrubs and grasses ignited at the fall of a cigarette or a broken bottle. Smoke half obscured the northern hills, rolling like cannon fire between their clefts, and the town streets, even the house interiors, were pervaded by the faint miasma of burning.

Without a newspaper or radio station of its own, the town floated on a groundswell of hearsay. The two national journals (which arrived a day late) printed articles whose brevity and plainness illuminated nothing. But everyone could see that the drift of farmers into the streets had swelled. Some of them still trucked out to their fields or herds during the day, and returned at sunset. But others had abandoned their ranches altogether, and set up in boarding houses or slept in the alleys on their horse-drawn carts, sprawled among the flotsam of their possessions. They were dour people, with sun-bleached hair and reddened hands. They did not look as if they would frighten easily. Almost all told tales of armed native bands and pilfered stock, or knew of some farmstead which had been attacked. But they had lived in isolation; their news was as fragmentary and filled with rumour and contradiction as the town's. Yet they seemed to accept the drought and savages with fatalism, whereas the townsmen, who had suffered less, were by turns panicky and outraged, and were demanding revenge.

Many of the farmers whom Rayner used to telegraph in the wilds now came to him from the streets. His clinic was already brimming with patients whose ailments were nervous or unspecific, and the hospital engulfed him half the afternoon in minor operations for an upsurge of accidents due to alcohol and heatstroke. Two babies in the hospital died of diphtheria. The humidity did not let up. The fans whispering under the surgery ceilings only redistributed the heat, and evening brought no touch of wind. The air banked up round the town in a wall of smoke and dust, and people began to feel that the seasons had stopped. After the sultry nights, everyone woke exhausted. Rayner slept only fitfully even when not on call.

Whenever he visited the old native, whose blood pressure remained erratic, he saw himself a traitor in the town's eyes. As he approached the copse where they were camped, he always hoped to find them gone. Yet he knew that the man was in no state to move.

'Who are these people?' Zoë demanded. 'Aren't they frightened?'

But the situation in the town seemed to stimulate her, as if she were at last witnessing something meaningful. She reported every rumour and incident. The night club closed earlier now, and she insisted on walking back alone through the near-silent streets, whose only danger, she said, lay in the drunken calls of the farmers from their wagons.

Then one night she returned tense with indignation. The half-caste dancer in the cabaret had suddenly disappeared, dismissed overnight by Felicie's father. He'd called the rest of the artistes together and explained that customers were commenting on the girl. It was bad for the club's reputation. You couldn't employ the enemy . . .

'Enemy! She was just a dancer.'

During the next few days Rayner noticed the last natives vanish from the town centre. Even the man who tended the plants in the mall was taken for questioning, and the girl on Nielsen's Baked Potato van disappeared one evening, and never returned. When Rayner enquired after them, people's fear surfaced in near-paranoia. There was no such thing as a civilised native, they said. 'Those people' always reverted to type.

The detection of half-castes had now become an ugly game. The darker-skinned townspeople fell under early suspicion, and people claimed to discern even in Italian and Syrian immigrants the savages' triple frown or the lines ploughing down from the bridge of the nose to the mouth's corners. You could tell 'them', people said, by their distinctive stance with their knees braced back, and by the way they walked on the balls of their feet, as if sneaking up on you.

Medical helplessness in face of the disease was changing people's perception of the doctors. They were suddenly seen as fallible. A cloud of disillusion brewed up, and an indefinable resentment. Rayner realised, too, that people were talking more personally about him. He was what the military termed an 'unreliable element'. Even the medical officer, his half-skilled analyst, had alluded to it. The story had spread that he had treated savages out of the bush, increasing the risk of infection, and had settled two of them in the parklands near the clinic. During his surgery Rayner sensed that even the older patients were troubled with him, although they said nothing.

It was Leszek – tremulous and brittle with pride – who broached the subject. 'Do you suppose that old man may be well enough to leave soon? It cannot be very safe for him now . . .' Even in this weather Leszek wore a linen jacket and tie, his white hair fastidiously smoothed back. But he looked stressed and pale.

Rayner said, 'His blood pressure's still too high.'

'I've never had to treat any of the savages,' Leszek said wanly, 'but they suffer from high blood pressure a lot, I've heard.'

Rayner knew what Leszek wanted. In his partner's face he saw the ghosts of the past assembling: fear of authority and of the community's hatred, the exile he never spoke about. Leszek's lips pursed primly, as if in self-judgement. Pride and fear were at odds in him.

'I'm having to regulate the man's tablets,' Rayner said. 'He doesn't even remember to take them.'

'The savages are used to their own medicines.' Again Leszek seemed to be saying: *They are not like us. Leave them alone.*

Rayner said, 'I don't want that old man's death on my hands.' But he knew, as he said it, that he was hoping Leszek would somehow absolve him from protecting the natives any longer. Like Leszek, he was growing deeply apprehensive.

'The trouble is . . .' Leszek nervously adjusted his spectacles. 'There's more than just the savages to consider. You must have noticed . . . you surely have. The whole clinic has become affected. Half the town knows. Only yesterday I was about to administer an injection when the patient asked, "Is that needle clean?" and I knew what she was thinking. Nobody ever used to ask that.'

It was true, Rayner thought, the patients who used to be so docile were suddenly questioning the sterilisation of needles and even of dressings. Only that morning a miner submitting to a blood test for lead poisoning had demanded to see the needle sterilised before his eyes.

'It's so much a matter of faith,' Leszek said. 'If people lose faith in us . . . if they start shying away from us . . . we'll kill people that way.'

Rayner felt a dulled, stubborn resistance to this. Leszek was simply afraid. 'It's ridiculous.'

Leszek said bitterly, 'People are ridiculous.' He took off his spectacles as if to obliterate his fellow men. 'But you can understand it. There've been seven whites killed here in as many weeks. What are they to feel?'

'I know.' The memory of those axed-in heads surfaced again. 'But the natives all come from different clans. This old man has no connection with the groups upriver.'

'I dare say not.' Leszek turned starchy and defensive. Perhaps he felt he was being accused of cowardice, or was accusing himself. 'But it's only a matter of time before the military takes the last of the savages in. And then what happens to them?' There was a tinge of reedy triumph in his voice. 'Yes, what then? It's better you tell them to go, before it's too late.'

That night Rayner was woken by confused shouts and cries. They sounded far away but violent, as if left over from nightmare, yet when he fully woke they were still there. He pulled back the curtain from a three-quarter moon. Beyond and a little below him, like a ghost over the blanched river, moved an unlit police launch. All along the near bank, where the last natives had camped, the darkness spurted lights and the screams and bawling reached him with unearthly distinctness. A cooking-fire showered the night with sparks before dying underfoot. A child was shrieking. But in that distance everything passed with a chill unnaturalness. Gradually the lights shifted downriver towards the road. Occasionally, in the flash of torches, Rayner discerned a jostle of heads as someone still resisted arrest. Then, one by one, the jeeps' headlights flooded the distant highway as they drove away, and the police launch drifted back into dimness. For a moment the loudest sound was his own breathing, short and harsh in the room's silence.

Then, with an eerie shock of familiarity, as if it resonated somewhere in his memory (but he could not recall where), there arose from near the river a long, disembodied howling, which wavered like a dog's under the moon, and died away.

By the time Rayner had tugged on his trousers and gone

outside, everything was silent again. He blundered along the crest of the slope, afraid of treading on a snake with his bare feet. He had forgotten to bring a torch, but by the time he reached the copse his eyes had adjusted to the moonlight. For the first time since their arrival he was praying that the natives would still be there. He thrust aside the branches until he reached the bloodwood trees.

They lay asleep on their quilt. The girl bunched on her side, her head covered by her arms. The old man's face was turned up to the sky. Yet he appeared not really to sleep. The converging lines which knit together his eyes and nose twitched and flinched at the air. And the big, dry mouth was never still. It uttered tiny cries. And he breathed so lightly. Rayner stared down at him with relief and something like affection. But in its enormous nest of hair the old man's face looked emptied, Rayner thought, as if he were the detritus of some older, sturdier race, which had lost its evolutionary way. And the cries he uttered were like the fragments of a language he had once known, and was trying in vain to recover.

15

How long the staff car had been waiting outside the clinic Rayner could not guess. The corporal had covered its dashboard with a blanket against the sun and fallen asleep inside. As they drove into the barracks he said, 'It was the captain wanted you,' and he pulled up outside the military police jail.

Ivar met Rayner in the warder's room. He was wearing a look of complicitous charm, and took Rayner's arm as if to lead him aside – but there was nowhere aside to go. There had been an unfortunate occurrence, he said. One of their prisoners – an elderly savage – had died of heart failure. The surgeon had carried out a post-mortem, but they needed a second signature on the Notification of Death form. It was routine, of course. He pushed the form across the desk until it lay under Rayner's eyes, then began to talk of other things. His relationship with Felicie was unexpectedly better, he said. And how was Zoë? Yes, she was certainly characterful. In fact you never knew which of her characters she was going to adopt next. This did make her . . . well . . . *difficult* . . .

The Notification of Death still lay on the desk beside Rayner's hand, with one of Ivar's pens beside it. Against 'Cause of Death', it read, 'Cardiac Arrest'. Rayner wondered: is he really expecting me to sign it without question?

'But of course Zoë is bright . . .' Ivar's smiles and laughter came and went, yet somehow made no difference to his face. It was as if his face were temporarily missing. Except that once or twice its eyes flickered down to the form, encouraging Rayner to pick up the pen.

In the end Rayner said, 'We'd better get on with the inspection, then.'

'Will that be necessary?'

'I can't sign an autopsy for a corpse I've never seen!'

'Of course not.' Ivar stood up. His smile was faintly disconcerted. 'I'm not familiar with the procedures.' Rayner realised, with surprise, that Ivar wanted his esteem. 'And the surgeon is absent at the moment.'

He led the way down a short passage and opened an iron door. The Intelligence lieutenant materialised behind them. Rayner found himself in a room which must once have been a cell. It reeked of chlorine. The body lay on a table in a linen sack. The lieutenant untied and eased back the cloth from the head and shoulders. 'He died about twelve hours ago.'

The man was no more than forty-five years old. His closed eyes made two dark-lashed crescents on his flat face. From the high cheekbones his features tapered to the natives' soft mouth and a tiny, withdrawn chin. It was an oddly humorous face, rather delicate. Its lines of pain − if that is what they had been − were all smoothed away. At any moment, it seemed, the eyes might fly open and the mouth crinkle into laughter.

Rayner pulled the sack from the naked body. The lieutenant fidgeted on the far side. Ivar stood behind Rayner, with the Notification in his hand. Rayner recognised no obvious sign of heart failure − the feet were unswollen − and there was no incision. He began to feel angry. How this native had died had been decided irrelevant. As for him, he was being enrolled as the army's pawn.

He asked, 'How did the surgeon arrive at his diagnosis?'

The lieutenant answered smoothly, 'I'm not sure.'

Ivar said, 'The man collapsed in his cell early in the night.'

It was difficult to detect bruising on the dark skin, but it appeared to Rayner that the whole region beneath the ribcage was heavily contused. A discoloration blacker than

109

the natural skin tone spread unevenly down to the man's crotch. It looked as if he had been systematically hit.

'How did this happen?'

For an instant the lieutenant looked confused, then his gaze followed Rayner's finger and he stooped down to stare. He said, 'He got into a fight with another prisoner.' But when Rayner looked at the lieutenant the watchful eyes and ambiguous lips no longer expected to be believed. They seemed simply to be saying, *Even if you don't cooperate, we'll do as we've decided.*

Then, when Rayner ran his hands over the native's skull, he encountered beneath the thick hair a sudden bulge. The skin was almost unbroken, but the tissue had thickened into a hard swelling ten centimetres across. And the surgeon had not even shaved his head.

Rayner straightened up. On either side, Ivar and the lieutenant had stiffened into silence. He said, 'I thought your man had performed an autopsy.'

'He didn't think it necessary,' the lieutenant said.

The Notification of Death rustled in Ivar's hand, but his smile had faded back into an expression of plastic concern. Rayner felt suddenly tired. If he didn't sign the form, it would make no difference. They would merely forge the papers, or suppress the death altogether. On the bare table the native's flared nostrils and soft mouth kept their hint of whimsical humour. But the frail-looking body accused him. He said: 'This needs a proper post-mortem – something I'm not qualified to carry out. The abdominal bruising could mean a ruptured spleen or several other causes of death. Most likely, in my opinion, he died from a fractured skull. So we need X-rays.'

Ivar said, 'That won't be possible.'

It was futile, Rayner knew, to argue. He said, 'Then there's nothing more I can do.' He turned and opened the door behind him.

Then Ivar touched his forearm, smiling, with the familiar

gesture which claimed old friendship, and handed him the Notification of Death form. For a moment the flagrancy of this so astonished Rayner that he took it. But in his erupting anger the treatment of the native and of himself were inextricably joined. He laid the form on the table beside the corpse's feet, and saw his pen tremble as it wrote in thick, jagged words: 'Cause of death: Cerebral contusion consequent on a head wound.'

Ivar took the form, and his smile vanished. The lieutenant was dragging the linen sack back over the body. Ivar said, 'You're making things more difficult for us.'

'You've made them impossible for me!'

Ivar began pacing back and forth in front of him, the few steps which the cramped room allowed. He appeared to be contemplating something, but perhaps just hated to concede defeat in front of the lieutenant, who was tying the neck of the bag in a neat double bow. It was only after the subaltern had left, closing the door which Rayner had opened, that Ivar said, 'I hoped at a time like this you would realise there was something more important than medical etiquette.'

Rayner said bitterly, 'I thought murder was what we were fighting against.'

But Ivar had turned cold. Rayner had the impression that his uniform had leaked upwards, into his face, and was slowly suffocating it. 'We're fighting for the peace of this town, perhaps even for its survival.'

'That's hyperbole.'

'Is it?' Ivar smiled just as he had done at school, when his secret knowledge turned everyone else stupid. 'We've received reports of armed savage bands numbering as many as fifty.'

'Then why don't you cope with them,' Rayner demanded, 'instead of . . .' – he waved one hand at the sack – 'this?'

'Because when we hunt them they scatter. That makes Intelligence vital.'

'What can they tell you? These people all come from

different regions.' Rayner tried to remember what the old native had told him. 'A few may be marauders, but the ones who drift into town probably come from other groups.'

Ivar said, 'In that case they know each other's movements remarkably well. Several have admitted to a plot to infiltrate and sack the town.'

'Was that suggested to them under interrogation?'

'I don't know. Interrogation isn't my job. But the lieutenant's not a fool.'

Rayner turned his back on the shape in the sack, as if it might be listening. 'People will admit to anything under torture. Just to stop the pain.'

'Nobody said anything about torture. Do you think I'd order it?'

Then Rayner realised that Ivar was angry – or as close as he could reach anger. His eyes had awoken in a controlled glitter. Perhaps this was no more than the simulated fury of army officers at insubordination, Rayner thought, yet even that suggested some discomfort in him, so that Rayner found himself thinking: he's vulnerable after all. Nobody on earth could be quite certain of himself.

It occurred to Rayner that the lieutenant had covered the corpse again on purpose: it would be harder to lie in its presence. He said, 'This man was beaten systematically. The heart attack attributed by your surgeon is pure fantasy.'

They were no longer facing either the corpse or one another, but staring at the cell wall three feet away. It had been thinly whitewashed over indecipherable graffiti. After a silence Ivar said, 'I don't think you care about this town. You've never felt any loyalty to us.'

His words threatened Rayner with all the certainty, the enclosed authority, of his own class and kind. That was their power.

'I care all right,' Rayner snapped. 'At least enough to hate this place losing its head.' And he thought at once, a little surprised, that yes, he did care about the town, about his friends and certain patients, about Zoë, even about the place's blind future.

Ivar said, 'But you betray it.' He edged the death notice into his inner pocket, slowly, as if giving Rayner a last chance to recant. 'You haven't changed, have you? You always did find some reason for being separate.' The words debarred Rayner absolutely, just as they had at school. He imagined his name appended to the Intelligence list of unreliable elements. 'It's easier for you to dissociate yourself,' Ivar went on, 'because you feel you don't belong here. You keep this pipe dream of returning to the capital. But people like me have to cope with the realities. It's rough going, but we do the best we can. We can't afford your morality. It doesn't work here.'

Rayner turned on him. 'You accuse me of idealism because I don't abet a murder! I don't have any morality I can lay my hands on, just hand-to-mouth decency. And sometimes not even that. I've never stuck even to medical etiquette. I've practised euthanasia like most doctors with a grain of pity in them.' He saw his own hands trembling; he stuffed them into his pockets. 'But I won't sign that form.'

Ivar looked at him as if at a baffling child, then turned his back, but found himself facing the corpse in its linen envelope. Again he seemed to be seeking self-exculpation as he said, 'These people aren't like us. They don't think like us. They don't share our sense of right and wrong. They – '

Rayner shouted, 'But they feel like us if you fracture their skulls!' He just wanted Ivar to stop talking, wanted the plastic mouth to stop going up and down, planting its rational syllables in his mind. It was Ivar's calm which was so dangerous, he thought, so insidious.

And it was true in its way, of course, the natives were different. When they came into contact with whites they fell instant prey to alcohol or disease. Yet out there in the wilderness they slipped back into collusion with something else, and appeared to live and die as if they did not

113

profoundly matter. They did not battle with life as the whites did. So they stayed backward, and were peculiarly still. They seemed to retain some secret which later peoples had lost. He remembered the paintings on the rock-face, their disembodied peace; but whether they imagined a future or portrayed a past, was impossible to say.

The echo of Rayner's shouting died in the tiny cell. It left behind a solid wall between him and Ivar, probably for ever. Before, the difference between them had been inarticulate, or the subject of banter. But now it had reared up with inescapable meaning.

Ivar opened the door, gently dismissing him, and said, 'None of this alters your obligation to the army if you're called on.'

It must have been Ivar's blandness, his imperturbable civility, which made it impossible to sustain anger with him for long. Rayner left the cell without answering, or looking back. As the staff car moved out of the barracks, he was disgusted to realise that his dominant feeling was regret for the loss of an old friendship.

16

That evening, as he walked home along the deserted river, he saw that the wreckage from the army raid still scattered the bank, as if nobody had been there since last night. But the last of the savages had gone. Their campfires had died to soft ant-hills of pure ash, or were smeared in a grey dust where the print of boots and bare feet overlapped. A torn blanket dangled from a branch. Some cooking pots gleamed under a bush. And once he came upon a necklace of tiny bones, broken, like vertebrae on the red earth.

In the clinic, when he had told Leszek that the army had tortured a man to death, his old partner had turned cold with recognition and said at once, 'Now you must see, don't you? You must tell that savage and the girl to go. You've done everything you can.'

'His blood pressure still swings over 210. He trembles all the time. If I let him go, he'll die out there.'

But Leszek only said, 'Better than dying in prison' – and the memories blanching his face lent him a cruel authority.

By now Rayner was obsessed by the two natives. For all he knew the army would seize them that night. An hour later, on the way to the hospital, he met the local priest, a stout man with frosty eyes, and told him that the military had cleared the river of savages, and what was he to do about his patient?

'In my experience these people are not converted by kindness,' the priest said.

'I'm not trying to convert them.'

'But judging by their actions, it's wrong and dangerous to harbour them. They're better among their own kind.'

In the hospital Rayner had approached the senior consultant warily, but the man had realised with a shock what he was asking. 'That's preposterous, Rayner! I'd no idea they were still there! You're not only jeopardising your own standing in the town, but that of the whole medical profession.' He had looked at Rayner as Ivar sometimes did, baffled and incredulous. Rayner began to feel he was going mad. The consultant demanded, 'How many people do these savages have to murder before you repudiate them?'

He passed a sodden quilt on the river bank, and a torn sandal; then he started to climb towards his house. Far to his left stood the copse of acacia and bloodwood trees where the natives were camped. He glared at it as he trudged up the slope. They would be sitting there, he knew, in their own impenetrable world, oblivious of the dilemma they were causing. He hunted for reasons to disown them, but found none. He prayed for them simply to leave. They were imposing on him an idiotic heroism or treachery. He might start to hate them. Yet he thought: this town's going insane about a sick old man and a girl.

By the time he reached his villa he had no anger left, just a bleak indecision. Zoë's cat was sitting under the porch in the fading sun. He turned into the garden to compose himself. The frangipani trees were dripping waxen blossoms into the brown grass, and all the canna lilies were in bloom.

After a while Zoë came out. In her flowered dress, with her hair loosed, she looked like the natural child of the place. But as she approached him her smile faded. 'What's wrong?'

He took her hand and began to walk. 'The army have just killed one of the native prisoners. They asked me to falsify the post-mortem, and I refused.'

'Ivar?'

'Not personally, I don't think. It was the Intelligence

fellows. My guess is the man fought back under torture and they killed him by mistake.' He stopped under the frangipanis, whose fall of flowers seemed somehow shocking now. 'There's not a native free in the whole town except the old man and the girl, and the soldiers may come for them any time. The old fellow wouldn't last a day in prison. It'd be torture enough to separate him from his daughter. And she'd be raped.' He kicked at the hard earth. 'But he's still so weak that if I send them away I can't guess his chances. He might survive, but he'd probably die.'

He turned to face her. Suddenly he realised how deeply, by laying this dilemma at her feet, he had put her on trial. He was not even sure what he wanted her to reply. He just stared into her face, whose vivid eyes overruled all trouble in it.

She simply said, 'Where shall we keep them?'

As he looked at her, standing under the milky trees, he was overswept by a boyish adoration. Quaintly he balanced her fingertips on his, and kissed them.

She laughed, startled. 'What's that for?'

'You.'

She stared back at him, puzzled. She did not notice that there had been any decision. 'Well, where?'

'I don't know. They should probably be in the back bedroom. It's sheltered from the road. We'll find them the moment it's dark.'

They stepped into the villa as if they were treading on glass. The huge, halting man followed the expressionless girl across the sitting-room to the far door. His whole frame trembled faintly as if it were independent of him, of the life sunk deep inside. Like a mariner between islands, he faltered from table to chair to window-ledge, but touched their surfaces only tentatively, as if testing their existence.

117

'You got a good place here, eh.' He held out a hand to Zoë. 'You Mrs Doctor?'

'I'm a friend.'

She showed them the kitchen. The girl stood behind her father, uncomprehending. But the man said, 'I remember these things from the cattle station days. I work these things okay, I explain to the girl.'

'But you tell us what you eat,' Zoë said. 'We'll buy the food.'

'Is okay for now. We got the flour. Some fruit. Whitefeller stuff make harder eating for us.'

The moment they entered the bedroom they went to the window and looked out into the dark of the garden. They murmured together. The trees seemed to comfort them. When the old man turned, he picked experimentally at the coverlets, the curtains, the cushions, but said nothing. His daughter did not seem to see them.

'If you go out,' Rayner said, 'don't go beyond the trees.'

The girl spread their quilt on the floor and squatted down. From her cord bag she drew out a long dish packed with tubers, two little bark spoons and a bone knife. Rayner watched her in fascination. She might have been alone. He had the impression that because for thousands of years her people had experienced only the wilderness and one another, a white face scarcely registered with her, and did not meaningfully exist. After a minute he and Zoë realised not that their own presence was intrusive but that they were simply no longer being seen, and they closed the door softly behind them.

But late that night Rayner was woken by something. He eased out of bed without disturbing Zoë. He heard the stutter of a distant motor, then nothing. As he parted the curtains and stared down at the river, he made out the dimmed lights of an army patrol among the trees. They went in utter silence, furtively. He watched as their lamps rose diagonally up the slope and passed before the house

118

without a sound. Then they dwindled along the crest of the ridge towards the bloodwood copse. As he gazed, they vanished and reemerged where the slope met the skyline, then one by one they disappeared.

During the following week the natives were so quiet in the house that Rayner often forgot they were there. All day, with scarcely a change of posture, they would rest on their haunches in the grass outside the back door, facing the trees. Sometimes the old man would doze off like this, bolt upright, his eyebrows descended like pelmets almost onto his cheeks. Occasionally Rayner would find him smoking hemp leaves in a little bamboo pipe, perforated like a flute. At first he moved to stop this, then let him dream in peace.

Meanwhile the girl squatted beside her father, weaving a basket out of pandanus fibre, or simply sat idle with her head faintly inclined to his. She never used the kitchen. Instead she built a cooking fire just inside the door. Neither she nor her father questioned the circular hole it burnt in the rug, but pulled their seed-cakes from its embers and sometimes offered Rayner a sweet fruit paste which they blended over its flames. In their room the beds and chairs were ignored, and they never touched an electric switch. Every dusk they unrolled their soiled quilt over the floor and slept back to back with their hair flared out around headrests improvised from the garden stones.

Yet they slept fitfully. Through the villa's papery walls Rayner heard their sudden words and cries. It was as if the stress which they denied by day was experienced in their dreams. Sometimes he felt it was in dreams that their real lives were lived, and that in daytime they merely waited.

The old man grew visibly robuster in these first few days, and even the girl began woodenly to acknowledge her surroundings. Whenever Rayner saw her she smiled at him,

119

but the smile was superposed on her face: she had copied it from her father. It flashed on and off. And when their eyes met, her gaze no longer dropped, but held Rayner's in a blank, unfathomable stare: just a pair of eyes, looking.

Rayner felt a premature sadness for her, because she might soon be alone, but his pity was impaired by her enigma, by the apparent absence of any person in her, and besides, she was not a girl any longer but a young woman. She had the long, veined feet and hands of her people, already refined, and her breasts pushed against the white dress. She knew no language but her own, yet Zoë befriended her with chatter – 'She must understand *something*' – and brought her different fruits and cakes, which were sometimes eaten and sometimes set aside.

Only the presence of the cat altered her expression. Then the knot of native unease flickered between her eyes, and when Zoë held the creature out to her she darted back in dismay. She did not understand what the cat was for. As Zoë fondled it, smoothing the paws against her own neck, the girl watched in wonderment, as if the cat and the white woman had a secret pact together.

On the second day Zoë heard a scream from her bedroom. She looked in and saw the girl sitting in front of the dressing table with her hands lifted to her head. She had discovered herself in the mirror. Until today she had used only a square of tin in which to glimpse her face, but now she was confronted by the brilliant, life-size woman who lived in reflection. She stared at her, awestruck. She steered her head from side to side, and pattered her fingertips over her cheeks. At last she realised that the woman would not suddenly do something on her own. Then, slowly, she unbuttoned the top of the torn dress, slipped it down from her shoulders and gazed at her reflected breasts. She laughed.

*

Now that in the town's eyes the two natives had drifted from Rayner's protection and back into the wilderness, he felt that people's stares were no longer on him (but perhaps they never had been). Yet the natives' presence in the house confirmed how little he understood them. They were not only different from the town's conception of its enemy, and from the axe-men of his own fear, but they were different from one another. The old man's years of stock-breeding had touched him with the white man's world. But the girl was a repository of her people's mystery. She existed free of any values he knew.

These days the town's anger and helplessness were palpable in the humid streets. Men shouldered their way to work as if the community's survival depended on it. Police and passing soldiers were routinely harangued. And the mood infected both the vigorous and the passive, depending on their fear.

From a long way away, as he returned from his rounds, Rayner glimpsed the elegant head of Felicie approaching along the mall. He expected her to flutter a hand at him and pass on, but instead her fists landed on his chest in a childish tattoo, and she drove him into a shop entrance. How could he have done that to Ivar, she demanded? Didn't he owe loyalty? Or else what was the point of old friends? With the town in the state it was, why couldn't he cooperate? He must take pleasure in sabotage, she concluded. He must want them all to go under. Otherwise, why?

Rayner said, 'The man had been murdered.'

'Ivar said he hadn't,' Felicie panted. 'And Ivar should know. Don't you trust him?'

'Not always.'

Her fists resumed their infantile thudding. 'You're his oldest friend!'

Rayner took her wrists and held her irritably away. 'It doesn't matter if I signed that death notice or not. The army would falsify it anyway.'

'Then why didn't you do it?' Her head shook on its neck like a flower. 'You're just stubborn.'

'Yes.'

'Why? Why?'

He pointed whimsically to his maimed foot. 'Because I can't run away.'

But Felicie refused to smile. She half screamed, 'Don't expect any loyalty from him!'

'I don't.' But Rayner wondered if Ivar were planning some reprisal.

'Because he has every right to grind you into the earth!'

'He hasn't any right to do anything. He just asked me to lie about a man's death.'

Felicie was close to tears. Her bouffant hair sagged like sodden corn. 'It's all right for you. You get paid by the state. But we're trying to run a business in this place, and everything was fine until now, just fine . . . until . . .' – her springing tears made her furious – 'until these savages had to start this killing . . . And *you* condone it. If this goes on the club will shut down. And what would happen to your precious Zoë then?'

But Felicie wasn't looking into Zoë's future, Rayner knew: she was looking into her own, and she saw nothing. He said curtly, 'Zoë's clever enough to get a job anywhere. She might start a new career.' Yet he could not imagine Zoë without her dancing. Her natural expression would be lost. So she was in the power of these people. 'Are things really so bad?'

Felicie crumpled. 'It's empty half the evening, Zoë must have told you. People come in early and leave their guns against the walls like it was an armoury, and go away by nine.' She shuddered. 'The farmers only make it worse. They don't even buy drinks, they just sit.'

She looked so abject, Rayner said, 'It will come right again.' He glanced at the suffocating sky. 'With the October rains.'

But as he went home, their conversation lingered uncomfortably with him. He wandered in the garden, breathing the faint, perpetual stench of bush fires, and at last came and sat beside the two natives. They were leaning forward a little, side by side, with their heartbreaking look of perplexity, saying nothing. They had perhaps been sitting like that all afternoon. The girl shot Rayner her confusing smile, then went indoors. The old man said, 'Nothing changed, eh?'

'You'll be well enough to go before anything changes.'

'I feel better than a long time now.'

They sat silent for a minute in the stifling shade of the trees. Then Rayner asked, 'The people here say the armed bands upriver are fifty or sixty strong now. You think that's true? What are they planning?'

'Maybe is true. Those fellows join together if they get scared. But those aren't my people and I don't know. That's hard territory up there, water-holes all empty in a bad year. That country dry out people in the head, and then they go killing.'

'Could they attack the town?'

'Those big groups not for fighting, I reckon. There's too many older fellows with them. Those bands just running scared. It's the lone ones do the killing.' He lifted his finger. 'Some of those blokes upriver gone bad singly, maybe, but they only kill a few folks.'

'They've killed eleven.'

The old man considered this in silence. His screwed-up eyes and forehead had retracted into a charred immobility. All his life seemed concentrated in the fleshy mouth, which moved in its beard like an independent oracle. 'Eleven not so many. Whitefellers'll come back and get those farms again.'

'The farms will be the same,' Rayner said. 'But you can't bring the dead people back.'

'People change,' the old man said. 'In twenty, forty years

123

people all dead anyway, and lying in separate graves. Me too.' He laughed. 'My life done now.'

Rayner revolted against his words, but could find nothing to say. As he stared into the native's cinder-coloured face, this acceptance of death no longer seemed the superstition which the whites claimed, but the knowledge of a people coeval with all this violent, ancient land – a people to whom death was only the flow of time and of the clan. That, perhaps, accounted for their stasis, their sometime indifference to killing. It made Rayner feel naïve. He could not share in it. He could only share the townspeople's outrage.

He asked the native, 'Have you killed a man?'

'I never had no reason.' The old face remained impassive. 'But some blokes I used to know, in the old days, they killed two, three fellers before dying.'

'Why?'

'Well, that was the custom, you know. He killed one of you, and you killed him. Fellers in those days didn't kill for land or stock. They killed for revenge, eh, for dead men. But I don't hold with that. Those ways gone.'

In the doorway behind them the girl appeared with a fresh-made cake in either hand. She darted forward to offer them, then sat down on the far side of her father and stared at the grass.

Rayner asked, 'Is she happy?' But as he looked at her, the concept of happiness seemed irrelevant.

The old man said, 'She'll be happy when we find our people. We been too long single.'

'You could leave in two or three days.'

The man said something to the girl and she answered back not in the shy tones which Rayner always expected, but in her harsh gabble.

The native laughed. 'She says you're a good man. You make her old father well again.'

'Remind her she must keep you well,' Rayner said. 'Tell

124

you to take tablets.' He looked at her enigmatic profile. 'She's a fine girl.'

The old man said, 'You like her?'

'You're lucky to have her.'

The native laughed again, comfortably, as if at something warm inside him.

Rayner asked, 'How far is it back to your people?'

'I not sure.' His chest heaved under its shirt. 'Maybe ten days, maybe fifteen. Our people too much scattered, they go out and live one there, one here, the young blokes.' He inscribed a circle in the dust in front of him. 'But the old fellers come back and die in their birth country.'

Rayner envied the man's freedom. In this nation, only the nomads moved about at will. If Rayner tried to return to his birthplace, he would meet a bureaucratic wall; but this man had only to walk. Rayner looked at the wavering circle which the native had drawn in the earth. It seemed a very natural journey. He asked, 'Where do your people go after they die?'

The old man answered at once, 'Some say you go into the ground, that you just rot there, and your life done. But others say you climb up the sky, back out of time.' He spoke as if both prospects were equal to him. 'I heard your white missionaries say that too, that some fellers sit underneath in the soil, other fellers sit above in the sky. It's the same with us.' He leant forward and smoothed away the circle in the dust with the palm of one hand. The girl watched him, as if this were in some way important. 'But I reckon maybe there's no way back into the sky, that since the tree got cut we stay down here.'

Rayner remembered the rock-paintings, in which a symbolic tree had separated the fluid figures from the static ones. But the photographs which he had taken of them had turned out wan. The camera seemed to have registered the painted scarp just as he first had: an empty wall of rock. But when he showed the photographs to the native, the

125

man's finger wavered across their surfaces in amazement and recognition. 'This the same place all right.'

In fascination Rayner tried again to pin down its story. Was this some inner landscape? Were the graceful figures the natives' ideal of themselves?

But no, said the old man. 'This just our life as it is, as it was.'

So their beauty was only an artist's convention, Rayner realised, mixed with the passage of time. 'And the tree?' He could barely discern it in the photograph; even on the living scarp, he remembered, it had been little more than a meander of faded white. 'The tree led into the sky?'

'That was in the old days,' the old man said. 'The sky was lower then.'

Dimly Rayner could discern the white divide in the photograph – and on its far side the region where the fluid figures turned plump and stationary. The old man's head sank onto his chest in a pillow of beard. 'Those ones belong before time.' He was growing tired, or perhaps reluctant. 'When the tree cut down, then time began.'

So the felling of the tree was the event which exiled earth from heaven: the start of mortality. Rayner asked, 'Might it grow again?'

'Some fellers think maybe,' the native said. 'And you can still see that place out there, the navel of the earth.' His hand lifted in the direction of the wilderness. 'Maybe one day the tree grow back.'

Rayner remembered the blighted stump which the old man had drawn him in the dust when they first met. 'How?'

But the man's head returned to nestle on his chest. He did not answer. Rayner had asked too many questions, he realised. Unwittingly he may even have probed the man about his own survival beyond death. The tree, after all, had been the avenue to paradise. Yet the man seemed to regard the future with a dispassionate familiarity. Perhaps

126

he was one of those who believed that the dead simply pass into the earth.

When Zoë met Rayner at the door next evening, she was holding a suitcase, and the cat was mewling round her ankles. She said, 'I'm going to the flat to sleep. I'm washed out.'

'Aren't you dancing?'

'I told them I can't tonight. The place is half empty anyhow.'

He heard alarm in his voice. 'What's wrong?'

Her recurring need to be alone had always taken other forms than this; he would sense it in the self-contained way in which she moved about the house, with averted head. But her turning-away tonight was tinged by petulance and accusation. In the oppressive heat, tiny bulbs of sweat glistened along her hairline, and she kept touching her knuckles against her eyes.

'I'm just tired,' she said. 'I've got period pains.'

He offered to drive her to her flat, but knew she would refuse. Then she said, 'I wish you hadn't been so superior with Felicie.'

He repeated irritably, 'Superior?'

'She's distraught about the club. It's becoming a desert, and she said you looked *pleased*.'

'I wasn't pleased.'

'You told her I could always do another job.' She stooped down and gathered up the cat. 'But I don't *want* any other job.'

Then Rayner realised what had angered her: he had belittled her vocation. And as she walked away down the road, with the cat glaring over her shoulder, she was flaunting her independence because she felt he had discounted it. He wondered, too, if the presence of the natives was starting to oppress her. Not that they imposed themselves – they were eerily quiet – but both Zoë and he had felt recently that the house was being watched.

They squatted outside the back door, as usual, in the sultry shadows. But the girl had changed. She sat very upright and still, with her hands spread in her lap. Across her forehead dangled a string of little green stones, and two circles of corkwood dye opened up her eyes into a black stare. When she shot her meaningless smile at him, the effect was of a portrait's canvas splitting. It brought a shock of emptiness.

Rayner sat beside the old man and took his blood pressure, which had been stable for a week now. 'In two days you'll be able to go.' But as he scrutinised the encircling trees, his relief was followed by a nagging disquiet. Anybody scaling the fence and parting the foliage might see the natives here. He said, 'You haven't noticed anybody watching?'

'My eyes not so good now.' The old man turned to the girl. 'But her eyes young, and she seen nothing.' He continued looking at her, while her painted gaze stayed fixed on her lap.

Rayner supposed he should remark on her, but her impact was unsettling. He said formally, 'She's looking pretty.'

The girl glanced at him, as though she understood. Then she and her father conversed together, he in a growling, sibilant flow, she in her abrupt jabber. They might have been speaking separate languages. The old man tapped Rayner's forearm; it was the first time he had voluntarily touched him. 'She says she's glad you like her.'

Rayner imagined this a native courtesy – and soon the girl got up and went into the villa. Behind them the sun had dropped like a red millstone into the mountains separating the town from the west. For the first time in weeks a shudder of wind arose, then stilled, and three bats came whispering out of the trees. Over the sky, too hazed and light for stars, the violet air was disappearing into indigo, and a trail of birds crossed out of the wilderness.

Then a small cry sounded from the house, and the old man said to Rayner, 'The girl want you to go in to her.'

Rayner did not believe that this was what he imagined. 'What does she want?'

But the native only repeated, 'She wants you to go to her.' His expression was lost under its blue-black skin.

Rayner got up, mystified. He went past the cooled fire in the annexe and entered the room. In a corner glowed two rush candles. The girl had taken off her headband and was combing out her hair with a wooden comb. As she turned her stare on him, the loosened hair fell short and thick round her face. For a moment she stood looking at him. Then her hands lifted to her shoulders and she matter-of-factly eased the white dress down her arms and dropped it to the floor.

Their misunderstanding was complete.

Momentarily her body, backlit by the candlelight, was visible only in silhouette, but Rayner felt a rush of anguish at her humiliation. He took the two steps to her and began 'Look . . .' He was about to tell her she was pretty, but that he could not touch her. He had forgotten that they knew no word of one another's language. His hands came up and held her shoulders, and he tried to look into her face. But she gazed back unfathomably. He had thought of her as a girl, but of course she was a woman. He supposed she had made herself pretty for him. She was wearing only a plaited cane armlet, and she smelt of sandalwood grease.

Her body was now fully lit in the weak light. It was lissome and coppery. Her young breasts brushed against his wrists. Her closeness had become unbearable. His fingers were kneading her shoulders, despite himself. He had an idea that by this – their only common language – he was telling her that he admired her, but would not sleep with her. But she just stared through her black-circled eyes,

129

waiting for him to begin, while his desire and his torment at her innocence mounted.

It was as if only her movements – fleet and sudden – expressed her. She darted to the bed and lay on it, her legs a little apart, her face tilted at the ceiling. The shift of light woke a glistening patina over her skin. He could not tell if she wanted him at all. Perhaps her father had persuaded her to it. Was it an act of gratitude, some kind of repayment? He had no idea.

But even on the bed she looked darkly natural: a barbarian body which clothes had insulted. He stooped over her, shaking his head – but even this sign-language was unknown to her. His unbuttoned shirt dangled above her breasts. His need had become a torture. He heard himself say, 'You're beautiful.' But she stayed inert. Only the savage's perennial knot of puzzlement was exacerbated by the candlelight.

Then he straightened beside her. She was not beautiful, or ugly, or anything he understood. He might only turn her into whatever he wanted her to be, his own untruthfulness. As for the girl herself, she was merely waiting for sex. It was perhaps something simple to her, uncorrupted by love. And he was as much a mystery to her as she to him, so that suddenly he saw himself in her eyes: a white anomaly whose head was oscillating inexplicably.

He stood up in the hot room and went to the door. Behind him the girl ran across to her dress. When Rayner reached the garden he was surprised that night had not come. But only a few minutes had passed. The same three bats were flickering overhead, and the old native's posture had not altered. Rayner said gently to him, 'Tell the girl she's very pretty, but that our customs are not the same.'

In the dark he could see no change in the old man's face.

17

The people imagined the town ringed in a circle of fire. The distant conflagrations blurred every skyline in grey-blue smoke, and tinged with ash the perennial dust which seeped in from the desert. It was impossible to tell how much the suffocating heat arose from the surrounding fires and how much from the unchanging sun. By day the air waited like a physical load to be shouldered or penetrated. At night you could see the flames glinting among the foothills or far out in the wilderness, like the camp fires of an army.

Almost nobody ventured beyond the town's confines any more, except with a military escort. Rumours spread of war parties one or two hundred strong, looming and shifting behind the smoke curtains. Where each main street dwindled into the wilderness, the army had set up an earth redoubt mounted with a machine-gun. These were tactically useless, since the suburbs could be penetrated from anywhere, and were meant simply to reassure. But in the end they only deepened people's sense of siege and quickened the creeping terror that was slowly paralysing all the town's arteries.

But when Rayner was ordered out again on army secondment, he found a confusion of evidence. Some farmsteads had been looted so thoroughly that even their timbers and steel fittings had vanished; others had been gutted by bush fires. But many stood strangely untouched. Poultry still strutted in their abandoned yards, and their doors and windows swung open as at their panic-stricken abandonment, giving onto rooms where the crockery was neatly stacked and food decomposed on the tables.

People now became afraid that the railroad to the capital would be harassed, and their last link with civilisation severed. Already the desertion of the farms had increased the town's dependence on food railed in from the coast, and prices had soared. An upsurge of nightime lootings was attributed to savage infiltration, but turned out – whenever uncovered – to be the crimes of hungry farmers and the exasperated poor.

Yet the municipality issued no new law and the military imposed no curfew. It was as if everybody knew what was expected, and obeyed rules against the savages more total than any that might have been issued. The municipal notice-boards were stuck with photographs of native atrocities – murdered farmers, pillaged ranches – and everyone assumed that savages would be turned in on sight. In early September a group of townspeople caught three unarmed natives prowling on the outskirts, and butchered them. Such was the mood of the town that their killers were cheered in the streets.

Among the town's youth, too, an ugly force of auxiliaries had risen up – roving vigilantes in blue armbands, who patrolled the night streets armed with clubs. These days they were almost the only people to be met with after dark. The few others who ventured out often carried rifles – armed not only against the natives, but against the farmers whose wagons crowded the alleys two abreast.

In Rayner's clinic the victims of the 'savage disease' were multiplying. Sometimes they came secretly, after surgery hours; and most would claim at first to be suffering from some other ailment. He grew to detect them by the vagueness of their declared symptoms, until in an outburst of nerves they would unbutton their blouses or shirts. '*What is it, doctor*?' Then they watched his face in terror. Compulsively they would run their fingers over the rash, but did so delicately, because it was raised a little from the surrounding skin and they were frightened it might spill over. The

132

simpler or franker among them wondered aloud if they had contracted it from some native they had brushed against three, six, twelve months before.

Dutifully, to comfort them, Rayner would investigate these patients' rashes, their mouths' lining and eyeballs, and so simulate control. A few scientific definitions and prognoses temporarily quietened them, but he could administer only placebos, and the malaise accompanying the rash was often indistinguishable from the lassitude inflicted by the weather. In the end he might only treat their fear. The symptoms should abate when the humidity let up, he said; and the causes were under investigation. Even local foodstuffs were being analysed. The disease was a mystery, he told them, but mysteries were sometimes benign. It betrayed no one's personal history, carried no stigma.

But one morning a suicide was cut down from under the town bridge, tainted with the rash from neck to scrotum.

To Rayner the disease was like a warning. It was waiting, as if its victims had been marked out. And he wondered superstitiously about a common factor among them, as though, after all, they had been morally branded. But there was none.

He must be growing imbecile, he thought. This sultriness was turning everybody's brain. Perhaps his sessions with the analyst were muddling him. Especially in the half-sleep of the nights, fragmented by dreams, his anxieties mushroomed. He dreamt of Ivar. Ever since their schooldays Ivar had been in control of things. Now Rayner had slipped beyond his grasp, and Zoë too – Zoë was perhaps the only woman who had eluded him. Yet even at school there had been a price to pay for not joining Ivar. 'Rayner won't swear the vow! Let's hunt him. We'll hunt you, Rayner, if you don't swear the vow.' The dream pattered with fear. Ivar wanted Zoë back. The Intelligence thundered on his door.

Awake in the dull pessimism of morning, Rayner knew that Ivar might plan a limited retribution. It would be nothing so feeling, so hurt, as revenge — that would be superfluous — just an appropriate measure to show where power lay. If the two natives were discovered here, Ivar might even have him imprisoned for a day or two, calculating to humiliate him before Zoë. In his blacker moments he suspected that only his knowledge of the major's disease prevented his arrest.

One morning, under the trees by his villa gate, he came upon a litter of cigarette stubs. Somebody must have been standing there, chain-smoking, watching the house hour after hour.

The night before the natives were to leave, he went into the street and began to walk around the compound. Now that cars and passers-by were so few, the antiphonal howling of the guard dogs filled the dark, and he could even hear the two-note bark of the desert owls. A single lamp shed an amber pool beside the road. The scrape of his lame foot jarred on the tarmac; then he turned along the barrier of his own fence and trees. They sent up a wall of darkness. He saw no one. A fit man could scale the fence, he knew. He scaled it easily himself. Inside his perimeter, the air was sick with frangipani blossom. But there was nobody. An upper window showed a curtained light, where Zoë had returned. Probably no one had been out for hours, and the natives were sleeping. He felt a foolish absolution. Above his head shone smothered stars.

When he went indoors he found Zoë half undressed before the bedroom mirror. Her cat was reestablished on its cushion in one corner, and her open suitcase spelt forgiveness. She looked at him teasingly. 'Where have you been?'

'I was checking to see if anybody was outside.'

'Somebody was. He walked off as I arrived.'

'That must have been me.'

134

She burst into laughter. 'That's ridiculous! I know your walk. This was a small man, on the far pavement.'

Rayner did not want to think about it. He kissed her mouth to stop it talking. But their eyes met in a moment of foreboding. He asked, 'How was the club tonight?'

Zoë dismissed the menace with her sudden ebullience. 'The club? Oh, you'd have *loved* it. There was *nobody* there! A few farmers and some bored vigilantes looked in early, but by the time I danced you could've heard a mouse yawn. You'd have been thrilled.'

Rayner said testily, 'I *don't* want the club to collapse.'

'No, not to collapse exactly' – she stepped mockingly up to him – 'but just to *fold* very genteely, so your girlfriend will be forced into a respectable job.'

'You'd never be forced into anything.' He held her away from him while his gaze travelled over her half-dressed body in a kind of penance. He was reminding himself of her again – a beauty more elusive than the native's – and concentrating his desire, almost formally, on her whiteness. He drew her against him.

As he kissed her, his fingers spread behind her shoulders and touched an area of faint, upraised roughness. It was familiar from many other bodies.

She felt him start. Her eyes followed his stare. He crushed her against him again, clasping her head to his chest. But she pulled away and stared down.

Out of her left armpit, but stopping short of the breast, crawled a thick crescent of chocolate. Slowly she lifted her arm. It curled beneath it, then broadened to an oval behind, lapping her shoulder blade.

She lowered her arm softly and looked at him. Her lips were tensed back from her teeth. But she only said, 'Well, that's it.'

She was chilled into calm. She did not want to be touched, he could tell. She just wanted to stand there, absorbing the knowledge of it, separate. But he began quaking inside. His voice, almost audible, pleaded in his head: *not her*. He said, 'There's no evidence it's dangerous.' But he was saying it more to himself than to Zoë. They had discussed the disease often, as if it were something which only others would contract, and she had heard everything he knew. Somehow he had never imagined it touching her. She was so vibrantly healthy. Even the purity of her skin seemed to deny it. He wondered: how on earth hadn't she noticed it? He held out his arms to her, but she turned her back. Then, realising its splash on her shoulder blade, she swung round again and covered her armpit with one hand. She said, 'It might be contagious.'

He saw the shame shaking her. The rash confirmed her ugliness in her own eyes. It was a natural eruption from the unsightliness deep in her, the inner blemish she believed in. She was challenging him to touch her.

He said, 'Have you felt ill?'

'I thought it was my period pains. It's nothing much.'

His hands alighted on her waist, then gently, consciously, slid up to caress her under her shoulders. He wanted to kiss the rash, to involve his fate in hers, in spite of everything. But she suddenly lifted her arms in an impertinent dance. She cried almost angrily, 'Christ, what's the fuss about? Nobody's died of this damn thing, have they?' She peered at it over her shoulder. 'And I can cover it up when I dance.' She made light of it with a harsh, impetuous gaiety. 'I expect I'm in the majority by now! We'll all have it in a minute. Why haven't you got it? It'll be the town's trademark! People who don't have it will be considered ill . . .'

But later that night Rayner fell victim to the panic of his most ignorant patients, wondering about her over and over, lying awake through silence in a sweat of apprehension.

18

All day before the natives left, the tension of their conceal-
ment and of his betrayal began to lift from him. They were
blameless: yet he longed for them to be gone. That evening
he found them still crouched in their grass and shadows,
but when he sat beside the old man, there seemed nothing
left to say. The girl did not look at him. And he perceived
her differently now. He was uneasily conscious of her every
movement, of her body's weight under the torn dress, even
the shifting of her woman's hands. Neither he nor the old
man spoke of her.

Rayner reminded him of his pill regimen: the bromide
tablets were in the girl's bag. It was futile to pretend that
the native might return for treatment. Then at dusk, just
before she left for the night club, Zoë brought out a coral
bracelet which the girl had liked, and fastened it round her
wrist. The girl gave a little cry, and flickered her arm back
and forth in delight. Almost for the first time, she laughed:
a soft, high sound like a bird trilling.

Beyond the gate, as Rayner went out, a man was reading
a broadsheet under the street-lamp. But by the time Rayner
returned from reconnoitring the road, he had gone, and the
last light had drained from the sky.

It was time to leave.

The car which Rayner shared with Leszek was a sturdy,
anonymous saloon, whose improvised blinds shadowed its
interior even by day. Seated side by side in the back, and
obscured by straw hats, the two natives looked indistinguishable from farmers. But the girl sat bolt upright,

paralysed. She had not travelled in a car since their days on the stock-farm, the old man said. As they started, she gazed transfixed. The needles wavered over the dashboard; the headlights threw weak blobs into the dark, and the streets began to unfurl in a placeless network of bungalows. There was no one to be seen; and no car followed. A few lit windows hung up in the dark. Once or twice a guard dog rose snarling from a garden.

Then, as they neared the town centre, stucco walls reared up and narrowed into alleys. The car's engine roared and echoed. Its headlights wobbled over flaking façades violent with graffiti. But the natives could not read. Once they steered down a gauntlet of farmers' wagons where lights and singing rose from makeshift tents and whole families sprawled asleep among their salvaged clothes and trussed poultry. A man lurched drunk from his cart into the headlights, jolting the car to a standstill. His face came up angry against the glass close to the natives, then dropped away uncomprehending.

'I've locked the doors,' Rayner said. 'They can't get in.' He could not tell if the natives' immobility and silence were due to fear.

They emerged into open space and skirted the Municipality, where a pasteboard clock face announced the times for public water use, then they crossed at last to the town's far side. Only two cars passed them, and a military jeep; and once the flashlights of a patrol overlapped the pavement as if to flag them down, but withdrew.

The street-lamps petered out. Beyond the roofs a profile of foothills showed blacker than the sky. The old man looked up and murmured. For the first time Rayner felt confident they would leave the town unscathed. They entered a district of warehouses: compounds of barbed wire whose gates were padlocked and barricaded. A posse of vigilantes spilled from a side road and stared at them in confusion. They branched down an inconspicuous street

138

then moved forward without lights. A few minutes later the buildings stopped dead and the tarmac turned to dust. They heard nothing. The place was too obscure to be overseen by an army post. On one side was a gentle swell of hills, on the other lay wilderness, and above them there opened up an uneven furnace of stars, which faintly lit the track ahead.

Rayner switched on the headlights again. 'You'll tell me where to stop?'

'I know the place. Is not far.'

The track could not have been used for months. The wheels purled along an artery of sand and tiny, reddish stones, and rustled over dying thorns. But in the wilderness ahead of them flickered a horizon of broken fires, so distant that their flaring and dimming seemed indistinguishable from stars. How did people live out here? There seemed to be nothing but saltbush and acacia, and sometimes the white trunks of eucalyptus trees glimmered like planted bones.

But Rayner sensed the natives quicken behind him. They were coming home. Their straw hats were gone and their faces, each shadowed in its canopy of coarse hair, had come alive, and were watching. They exchanged short, quick sentences. Whatever happened in the old man's body, Rayner thought, he would feel better here.

By now they seemed to have been travelling a long time, and the path had almost faded. Sometimes the headlights scattered groups of gazelles, and once they came upon a file of long-horned cattle standing asleep across the track. A kilometre beyond, the blackened shell of a farmhouse appeared. And beyond that, nothing.

A few minutes later, where a cairn of stones marked the way, the old man said, 'Now we go footwalking.'

They clambered out into a sudden hush. On one side the foothills showed stark; on the other was wilderness. The air shrilled with cicadas and the sky was awash with stars. They stood awkwardly together. Rayner did not know how to say goodbye. He might have clasped the girl's hand, but her arms circled the quilt and water bottles, and she was already gazing along the hills where they would go.

The old man lingered by the car door, but his body seemed less a burden to him now. His breathing filled it. He was fumbling inside his shirt, and at last pulled out a necklace of mussel shells which he thrust against Rayner's chest. In the dark of his face and of the night, Rayner saw his smile gleam. He realised that he would miss him. He even experienced the unaccountable sensation that the savage had always been with him, but was now going away. The mussel shells glimmered in his hands. He had nothing left to say. But he reached out and took the old man in his arms.

As the natives moved out of sight, following the lea of the foothills, Rayner wondered how far they would have to go. They seemed to be walking into nothingness. Their slow, private dignity no longer struck him as strength, but as a kind of melancholy, and the two dark shapes merging with the plain looked suddenly vulnerable.

19

Rayner had anticipated his aunt's letter for so long that when he returned from work next evening and found it, he was seized by apprehension that it would not contain what he had hoped.

Written in a faltering parody of her old hand, her words dropped to him out of another realm. The arrangements for transferring her house to him were almost complete, she wrote, and she hoped he could meet her lawyers soon. His temporary residence permit was enclosed. She did not know how he regarded his future, but her friend Dr Morena was seeking a junior partner, and she had made bold to mention Rayner's name. She thought the partnership a pleasant one, and the indefinite extension of his permit would only be a formality. She imagined that Rayner would not lightly give up his present, thriving practice, but perhaps he would write to her? She had less than six months to live.

He read the letter again then folded it into his shirt pocket. This old woman, whom he scarcely remembered, had in his eyes acquired magical status. A frail, dying lady in bombazine and a toque hat – yet one push of her bony hand, and the wall of government control had gaped open. How had it happened so simply? Perhaps the network of state repression was loosening at last, and he had not known.

He walked light-headed in the garden. The torrid summer had hammered it into a rectangle of brown. Even the hibiscus hung prematurely withered. But October was near, and perhaps the autumn rains, and in the darkening air a gasp of breeze sprang up and died. Outside the back door, the natives' departure had left a crescent of crushed grass. Inside, Zoë had cleared away the cinders from a charred circle in the rug, and a column of soot still radiated to the ceiling.

It was Zoë who concerned him now. The sun had set, and in an hour she would return. He went into the kitchen, found some bread and fruit, and waited for her. His elation contracted inside him. He suddenly resented his own passion for her. For years he had dreamt of his return, and now it was darkened by this violent, wayward love for a woman who had abandoned any wish to return herself. And he dreaded his own pity, his regret. She'd known from the start that he intended to leave; but he'd told her one thing with his mind, and another with his body. They had never talked of marriage, yet despite everything it had hovered in his thoughts. He had the idea that if he'd known her in another place, perhaps as a young girl in the capital, then they might have made a future. But now, in her earthiness and stormy disenchantments, she belonged here.

He could not take her back with him.

Then he became alarmed by his own fear of loss. It welled up inside him like nausea. He tried not to think of her. He hated his own weakness, if that is what it was. He realised, even in the kitchen, how his surroundings had become hers: the choice of food, the herbs, the fruit baskets, the capricious cat. He kept his eyes on his meal. He tried to avoid his own sorrow by thinking of her future. He could not envisage it. She was only twenty-eight; yet often people were overawed by her. Her exuberance and naturalness attacted them, but there was something else – mercurial and perversely independent – which fended them off.

As the door opened, he could not anticipate her mood. It always played on her face, and was governed by the reactions of that coarse audience to her dancing. But tonight her eyes were on him. 'You've had good news.'

'How did you know?'

'You're looking guilty.'

Then he told her. He told her about his aunt's illness and that he'd soon return to see her; and yes, he would accept the medical partnership, and the house. The opportunity would never come again.

As he spoke, his tone grew harsh against its own apology, and his gaze lifted from the table to her. But she had slowly turned away from him was was facing the blackwood dresser hung with crockery. She said, 'I ought to be glad that you'll be happy.' But the dresser clinked faintly, as if trembling under her hands.

'I don't know about happiness.' He sounded strained and suddenly futile.

Then her gaze was on him. 'So you'd desert the town and your practice for that place?'

He tried to retrieve his own harshness. 'The town doesn't need me. The October rains will be here soon, and then all this madness will fade away. If I could cure the disease, I'd stay. But I think it will cure itself.' He felt his voice falter and reach out to her, but she had turned her back again. 'I think it's benign.'

He was sick with himself. He had momentarily forgotten about the disease, her secret rash. He'd persuaded himself that the epidemic was transient. But he couldn't know. He wanted to touch her, but guessed she would wrench away, so he went on sitting in front of his half-eaten meal, which suddenly looked gluttonous. He said, 'Leszek will be all right. He has two younger doctors wanting to join the practice.'

But Zoë's back had hunched as if against a sandstorm, and in its thickened bulwark it seemed to hold all her dashed pride and growing resentment. Her anger was seeking a conduit, but had not found it. Not the town, no, nor Leszek. It was not them that he was so violently

143

deserting. She said in a brimming voice, 'Did you always know you'd leave me?'

'Yes.' The moment he said this he realised that it wasn't quite true, but it seemed better not to tell her now.

'That must have been strange.'

Yes, he thought, strange and terrible. Yet while you were living the relationship, even with the prospect of eventual betrayal, it seemed natural. But he could not explain to her this waiting to return, this knowledge that completeness lay somewhere else. Zoë did not understand that kind of thing. He said, 'You knew I'd go back to the capital. I always said so.'

She turned round now. Her face was gaunt. 'I didn't believe you'd go on preferring a place to a person.'

'It's not just a place.' He despaired of explaining to her. He himself was beginning not to understand. When he asked himself, *Why? Why?* he was answered only by an immense, irrational yearning. He said, 'It's like being . . . whole again.' But her face was an angry blank. 'It's my past. I felt natural there.'

'Aren't you natural with me?' she cried. 'But I suppose the girls are better there, with their swanky clothes and accents.' She hovered above him trapped between fury and sadness. 'I don't understand you! When you're with me, I feel you're mine. But when you're on your own, God kows what happens to you. I think you just forget. Do you? What happens?' Then her anger overflowed. 'I think you just go cold, like a snake back in water! You accuse this town of materialism, but why are you leaving it? Because you want a new job! And a grander house and a suitable girl!'

'I'm just going where I'll feel committed. It's a finer place than here.'

She said stubbornly, 'I don't remember that.'

'I do,' he said, 'and if I could get you back there, I would.'

She almost shouted, 'I don't want the fucking capital! I want *you*!' Then, as if she too despaired of being understood, she turned cynical. He'd never heard her like this before. 'That charming city! When I was last there they threw out all the prostitutes and dancers' – she executed an obscene pirouette in front of him – 'probably all the artists too, anybody who'd suffered anything, so they were left with the most *beautiful* city, full of children, I expect, with a few angels and mutes. You'll *love* it . . .'

Rayner said cruelly, 'You mock it because it rejected you – or you rejected it.'

'Oh *yes*. I wasn't good enough for it. I had to be got rid of, like a germ. Now that I've been gone ten years, it must be *ever* so pure.'

But when he looked up at her expression, Rayner saw a familiar desperation: her ferocity against herself, the conviction of her inner worthlessness. And in this moment of disclosure he realised that she did, in some part of her, want to return, but could not, and he was racked by guilt and sadness. He was abandoning her, diseased, to a failing job in a fear-ridden community.

'But Zoë . . .' He wanted to tell her he did love her, but the words shook on his lips and would not come out. He had no right to tell her anything.

She glared at him and cried, 'Don't you bloody pity me!'

Then he reached out, pulling her against him, and kissed her mouth. She twisted it away from him, but he kissed her cheeks and hair, as if this was all that was left to him, and she slowly relaxed in his arms. Eventually she murmured, 'I'm all right, I'm all right,' but her voice strayed into trembling, then she sat on the floor and the tears coursed down her cheeks. He knelt beside her, rocking her, while she buried her face on his chest. He found himself repeating like a prayer, 'If only you could join me,' but she simply answered,

'What would I do there?'

For several minutes they sat together without talking,

145

exhausted. The cat came and curled itself round them. Zoë said, 'When will you go?'

He steeled himself. 'In a couple of days. I'll be back in two weeks . . . to clear things up.'

'So quick.' She ran her fingers over the cat's fur with a little broken laugh.

Then her head returned to his chest and he could sense, rather than hear, the renewal of her weeping, like a deep, sighing storm, which shook her body with regular convulsions, whose epicentre lay far inside. It was as if she were crying not only for him but for her broken past, her lost parents, her dead child. He had no way left to comfort her. He was numbed by the depth of her grief.

She whispered, 'Damn you.' He cradled her against him. Sometimes she might have been asleep but for the clenching and unclenching of her fingers in his shirt. He wondered how soon she would resurrect, but as he did so she became two women in his mind. The vibrant, dancing Zoë, he thought, would revive tomorrow. But the one in his arms, whose face had been thinned away by tears, the one without self-belief, she might not exactly recover at all, but store him away in the pantheon of her failures, as proof of her valuelessness. When he tried to see her future, he could not. It even crossed his mind that she might return to Ivar. And he could not predict how much – over how long a span – he would yearn for her.

He asked, 'What will you do?' as if she might somehow change course.

'I suppose I'll go on in that place, dancing.' Then she added, 'But you won't be there.' She seemed to have to remind herself of this, cruelly, out loud. 'I expect I'll start to hate it, remembering what you thought of it. If only there were windows down there. But there's no light. And it's true, they're pathetic, those girls, Felicie and the rest. They're ill half the time, all just hoping for a break one day, a decent man, or any man. There's not one of them happy. But they seem to need me, and I try to like them . . .'

She was talking of her loneliness, but too proud to give it that name.

'I'm sorry.' He'd never heard her speak so sadly of her work.

'If you were sorry, you'd stay.' She said it bleakly, drained of resentment. Just a fact. Then she stood up. 'I'm going home.'

The word 'home', as she spoke it, was filled with a bitter self-comforting. 'Home' before had always meant here.

'You shouldn't go back alone.'

'Who's going to bother me?' She tried to joke. 'An old woman with a cat.' Her voice choked. 'Better leave me alone. I *am* alone.'

Rayner watched her pick up her bag and the cat, then hesitate, as if these were too few, and there was something she had forgotten.

Then she left.

20

The next morning a cloud appeared in the sky. The first in four months, it hung alone in the hazy blue. People poured into the streets to gaze at it, or emerged exclaiming onto their rooftops. How had it arrived? Where was it going? Above the smoke pall, it hovered crisp-edged and immaculate, and its solitude lent it the strangeness of a portent.

But little by little its silhouette smudged and it began to disperse into the suffocating ether. By noon it was no more than a vapour inexplicably blurring the sky, and soon afterwards it had gone.

At first it left in its wake an extraordinary depression. Staring up at it, people had entertained an idea that it might expand or multiply, then darken into rain. Now they just said, 'It's gone,' and were struck by an irrational hopelessness. But later, hours after it had vanished, they were still scrutinising the sky for signs. Their gloom at the cloud's evaporation was slowly replaced by the memory of its mysterious arrival, and they began to say, 'It's got to mean something. There must be more.'

Soon after dawn Rayner had noticed it sailing like a sign above the wilderness. It seemed to exonerate him: he was leaving the town with hope. Bruised by thoughts of Zoë, he planned the day as a mass execution of duties. Everything must be clean and fast. He did not want to encounter friends or even walk down the mall. So he kept his mind on practical things: seeing his sickest patients, telegraphing his aunt, booking tomorrow's rail ticket, briefing the locum who would replace him for two weeks. All day he consciously excluded from his mind anything which might touch him with regret. He wanted nothing to dim the elation of his going.

He tried to be brusque even with Leszek, but failed. When he told him that he intended to accept a post in the capital, the old man smiled with a faraway recognition. He'd have liked to retire there himself, he said – to the restfulness, the clement weather – instead of dying out here. But he said this without rancour, and Rayner realised that the concept of returning anywhere had faded in him. His past was too brutalised.

It was late by the time Rayner started home. He thought without nostalgia of his villa above the river. He would sell it back to the cooperative in two weeks' time. Only the return of Zoë's things would be bitter. He did not want to think about that. And as he approached the house he saw a rectangle of light suspended above the frangipani trees, and realised that she must be back.

Downstairs she had already gathered up most of her crockery and hangings, but left others among his, perhaps forgotten, or simply because they fitted there. Her bright wall-carpets were folded up on the kitchen floor. He wondered if she was angry. Then, on the table, he saw among his mail an envelope bearing the state military seal. The letter required him to report for a four-day expedition which would start the day after he returned from the capital. It was signed by Ivar. Rayner thought: so this is my punishment for getting away. He thrust it angrily into his pocket, then started inwardly to laugh. He did not mind. He did not mind anything Ivar did now.

Upstairs, Zoë had laid a few of her clothes in a case, then abandoned them. She had come across one of his old photograph albums, and was sitting on the bed, leafing through it. She smiled at him, composed. She said, 'I was beginning to think you'd gone already.'

'No, tomorrow.'

She was still fiercely made up from the club, her hair pressed back shining above her nape. A smear of glitter-dust winked round her neck.

'Did you make your arrangements?'

'Yes.' He sensed that she had gathered herself together for him, in pride or shame. 'You found my photo album.'

'I was looking at where you were going.'

He sat beside her, his hand on her knee. The album spread open on high, balconied houses and green parks behind wrought-iron railings, on friends dancing, or diving, or on picnics together. They were embalmed, of course, in perpetual summer, and everyone was smiling.

He said, 'It wasn't always like that.' But she went on fingering through the album, perhaps trying to understand, and he began to feel ashamed as these revelations of beauty and privilege unfolded before her, because her youth had not been like that. She had rebelled. But she looked at the photographs more in bemusement than in envy. Their world seemed far away to her; her nostalgia for the city, if that is what it was, had been severed from reality. Several times she pointed to people and asked who they were: Jarmila, Leon, Adelina smiled at the tip of her finger.

'Who's that?'

She was staring at Miriam on a picnic in a summer frock, pretending to be drunk. It occurred to Rayner that the irreverent photograph could have been of Zoë herself, ten years younger and more expensively dressed. But Miriam looked less real, ethereal almost, enclosed for ever in that time and place. Zoë said wanly, 'She's attractive.'

'Yes.'

'I suppose they're all rather grand, those people, and rich.' Her voice glinted with rebellion, but her face looked pale. As she leafed through four more years, she turned rather quiet, then closed the album up. She shot him her old look of intensity, of tenderness. 'Can you find that again?'

150

Then she stood up, as if to resume her packing, but instead faced him almost formally and said, 'I didn't mean to talk like that last night.'

He touched his hands to her shoulders. 'It doesn't matter.'

'It does matter.' She drew back from him, not in coldness or in anger, but to finish unimpeded what she had to say. 'I don't think much about the capital any more. I've got bad memories. But it matters to you.' Her voice trembled a little. 'For all I know, I'm running away. Perhaps the city would accuse me, because I've come down in the world. I never fulfilled my ambitions there, you see, all that ballet stuff. It was in the capital I first saw *Swan Lake*.' She pointed her balletic feet in an odd, cynical nostalgia. 'My parents would despise me now, if they knew.'

Rayner did not know what to answer. He felt perversely saddened that she did not long impossibly to follow him.

She went on, 'I didn't want you to think I despised you for going. On the contrary.' She picked up the photograph album, carried it across the room and replaced it in the drawer where she had found it, as if she were burying something. She said simply, 'You're better than me.'

He scowled. 'No . . .'

But she laughed at his expression. 'Anyway, the capital's just not my kind of place any longer. I couldn't last there.' She wriggled her shoulders as if reviving her circulation. 'I can manage here, even if that club does depress me sometimes.'

She stared out of the window into darkness, keeping her back to him so he could not see her expression, then said clearly, as if in words she had practised, 'You've got every right to leave.' He saw her fingers tighten on the sill. 'We never promised each other anything.'

For Rayner, watching her slight figure against the darkness, this was more unbearable than anything the night before. It wrenched him back to her, and filled him with a sad, furious frustration. But he did not know whether this anger was directed at himself, or at the intransigence of state law which would separate them, or at Zoë for her disruptive courage. He came behind her and linked his hands round her waist and kissed her.

She demanded whimsically, 'Shall I yell or plead? Then you can despise me.' She swivelled round in his arms and waggled her head comically in front of him. She was trying to drown her own grief as well as his. 'No, I'll torture you with the memory of my *beautiful* unselfishness.' Gently she unlocked his fingers round her, stepped away and began lifting down the pictures of owls she had hung near the bed. 'But I'm not leaving these. I can imagine your ritzy girlfriend in the capital asking, "Who on earth gave you those *vulgar* birds?" She laid them in the case. 'But *I* like them.'

'So do I.'

'Well you can't have them. You're so *serious*, I'm going to leave you something *absolutely useless*, to do you good.' She closed the case and pretended to ponder. 'The stuffed armadillo, I think.'

There was no more packing to do. The room looked bare, as if it had already been abandoned. Its ceiling fans rustled unevenly. In the square of night beyond the window, the red and amber lights of the smelter stack shone like planets fallen off course. Rayner was conscious of a hovering un- certainty in Zoë's movements, as well as in his own. He turned off a light, rearranged some books, removed his watch. When his eyes met hers, he did not know what to say. Out of his need and love for her, however constrained, and out of a sudden compassion which she would have hated, he wanted to make love to her again. But he had no right to ask, and his gaze swerved away from her. It was she, standing almost shyly on the far side of the bed, who said in a small, defensive voice, 'Do you still want me?'

'Of course I do.'

She did not look at him, but released her hair and dress

almost in one movement. Then he took her in his arms and she buried her lips in his neck. Once, as they lay together on the bed, she grimaced at the blemish trickling from her armpit, and murmured something in the lilting cadence of the capital which sometimes returned to her when they were making love. Softly he lifted her arm from the rash and kissed it.

In the past, he knew, she had sometimes separated his daytime presence from her night-time lover, closing her eyes and telling him not to speak, as if sex had to be anonymous. But recently this had changed, and she had looked and spoken back to him in this softened voice. It was as though the two parts of him – or of herself – were becoming one to her, and this private wound, which she could not explain, was healing.

But when she stared at him now, her eyes were brilliant and afflicting, so that he kissed away the accusation he imagined there, to close them. For an intense moment he lay motionless in her warmth, not wanting to end, and for long afterwards they stayed intertwined. But instead of tiredness he felt an inarticulate confusion. He became neurotically aware of the panting of the fans overhead, and of the dogs moaning in the suburbs. There was no trace of light in the room, and it was only by the closeness of Zoë's breast against his that he detected her silent, internal sobbing, and realised that her face was plunged beneath his into the pillow.

But later, while he lay awake, she fell asleep. Her breathing turned quiet, and his lips against her cheek found no new tears.

21

As the last bungalow lurched past his window, and the train moved north over deserted cattlelands toward the hills, Rayner was filled with relief. He watched the black streamer of the smelter stack fade beyond the engine's bluer smoke; and as the railtrack elongated and thinned over the plain, the vast, complex burden of the town seemed to loosen and slip physically away from him. Leaning from his empty carriage, he saw the last vestiges of habitation disappear: ghostly ranches and breached fencing. There was no sign of any savages. There was no sign of life at all. All the town's brutalising turmoil, its hordes of semi-exiles with their laden pasts, their paranoia, were dropping away like an aching memory below the horizon

At last he sat back and watched the wilderness passing across his window. Nothing moved in it. Over whole regions an immunising sweep of fires had charred the earth to a fine dust, and stripped and tilted the trees. To Rayner this forbidding land seemed to isolate his own past back in the town, and prevent it from following him. He took off his sweat-stained shirt and hung it in the window. As the hills lifted round the track, and the train laboured up between them, he felt as if all his imperfect adulthood, its half-loves and compromises, was dying behind him in that blighted country. Now, looking back on the plains, he could not glimpse the town at all, only a burnished waste where dead rivers went.

Then, in spite of himself, his head filled with Zoë. Imagined somewhere in the plain behind him, she suddenly seemed so localised and confined, and so far away, that he suppressed her with a choking sadness. He resented her for intruding on his elation. He waited for her face to leave him. But it did not.

The train had only four passenger coaches. For the rest, he'd noticed, its trucks were heaped with funereal-looking silver-lead ingots from the mines, and slushy piles of zinc concentrate. For hours the engine heaved these into the mountains with slackening gasps, and sometimes came almost to a standstill. Treeless palisades of rock circled the track, and long valleys hectic with scree and streams.

At nightfall Rayner stretched across his bunk in the suddenly cool air, knowing that dawn would find him less than three hours from the capital. The train roared and whistled in the dark. For all he knew he was lying in the same bed as fifteen years before, when he had journeyed into exile, sobbing because of Miriam – until the soldier in the bunk above had bellowed at him to shut up.

Now, staring up at the grimed ceiling, dulled by the drone and shudder of the wheels, he was stricken by the idea not that the capital had changed – fifteen years wasn't long in the life of a city – but that his memory had fatally enhanced it. Nothing, surely, was ever as you remembered it. He must have forgotten a great procession of ordinariness and squalor. Even his photographs, which recorded a city anointed in sunlight, were of course selective. He felt faintly sick. The streets and houses of his youth could not have survived as he imagined them. Lying sleepless for another hour, the wheels thundering in his head, he felt his misgiving slide gradually into blackness, until he conceived that all the remembered grace and gentleness of the capital might have belonged only to the sheltered childhood which he could never reenter.

Yet his memories were too few. People leapt and vanished in them like dolphins. Where, for instance, was the waif-like Anna who gave him the crystal he'd laid on the altar?

And Uncle Bernard of the coloured handkerchiefs? And when he thought of his old gang – Leon, Jarmila and the others – he knew he had lost contact with all of them, and experienced a vague unease. For in their different ways, they must have flourished more than he had.

He imagined them, for some reason, as refinements of their younger selves: Jarmila and Adelina with their blonde hair now fashionably short, married to affluent government officials. Gerhard, his youthful handsomeness matured, would himself be such an official, and Leon a successful but reclusive painter. And as for Miriam . . .

It must have been the engine smoke blowing through the carriage window in the early morning which made Rayner dream of the fire. The hands clutching the sheet at his chest became those of a five-year-old child. He watched his mother burst through the door and stand staring at him again, but he saw her more clearly than he had in life. The gauzy smoke had thinned from round her, so that her soot-smeared face smiled from an evaporated halo. But this time she did not come to him. Her hands were behind her back, as if tied. He woke up coughing from the smoke, and realised that the sun was up and glinting in his eyes.

The country outside had changed to scrubland and orchards. The train stopped at little torpid towns where half the men looked decrepit, and the women were out of sight. A few farmers clambered on board in wide-brimmed hats and shorts, lugging old-fashioned travelling cases labelled Slezak or Larsen or Bollack. They had sun-blistered legs and arms. Sometimes they disembarked enigmatically at villages of miners or rail-workers: white bungalows clean on their stilts around wide, single streets.

An hour later Rayner glimpsed the sea; then the southern suburbs of the capital gathered round and a minute afterwards the train was easing into the station. He disembarked onto the same platform – even, he imagined, the same space – where Miriam had never said farewell. As he swung his suitcase through the barrier, the police stopped him only cursorily, and stamped his residence permit without a question. The old tension seemed to have gone. He was not even asked to register.

As he walked out of the station, his dread that the city had changed enclosed him again. But opposite him, in the young sunlight, there rose up at once the terraced and balconied mansions he remembered, with their white-washed pediments and frail lunettes above the doors. The town he'd just left had grappled and swarmed over the earth, but this one hung the sky with a serene assembly of spires and gables. Even the colours of its façades were pastel blues and greys, blending with cloud and air.

His memory had held true.

The street where his aunt and parents had lived was barely ten minutes' walk away. He went there in a euphoria of recognition. He felt he was breathing deeply, fully, for the first time in years. The names of all the streets and squares came back to him, and of half the shops which ran out white awnings over the pavements. He might have been sleepwalking. The whole city – avenues, lanes, crescents – shimmered a little out of focus, as if his present-day eyes could not anchor it clear of his memory. At any moment, he felt, he might encounter his teenage self swinging down the street arm in arm with Leon or Gerhard. Yet the city now was inhabited by *other people*. It was bewildering.

He took countless detours on the way to his aunt. Sometimes he just sat on his suitcase on the pavement and gazed. After the rumbustiousness of the town, the restraint of passers-by was restful and a little strange. The cars never hooted. The height of buildings and the breadth of parks seemed to touch the inhabitants with quietness. Their history was remembered in statues, museums, even antique shops. He gazed with satisfaction at the Corinthian arcades of the State Assembly, and even at the corbels and lintels of

157

ordinary houses. He noticed more gardens, and the steepled brick and whitewashed churches were everywhere. He thought of sitting in a coffee house, just to savour the languorous sing-song of people's voices, but did not.

It occurred to him with astonishment that as a youth he had inhabited this place blindly – and soon, he knew, he would do so again. But for the moment he felt outlandish. He even tried to curb his flailing foot as he walked. His clothes must brand him an outsider, he thought. Yet nobody seemed to notice him, and the people were dressed little differently from those back in the town. A few men sported linen jackets and tropical suits, and the town's bush hats were replaced by panamas. Some of the women carried parasols and little gilded fans, which at first he thought an affectation; then he noticed, above everybody's head, a wavering column of gnats which neither settled nor went away.

He turned at last into the street he best remembered. It was unchanged. All the balconies and verandahs frothed with wrought iron, which trickled its shadows over the peeling walls. The façade of his parents' house had been repainted in café au lait, but he craned over its railings at the same garden of jasmine and roses. Their mingled scent, sharp with the tang of the distant sea, was the fragrance of his childhood. On the lawn two fat girls were playing.

He walked on seven more doors to his aunt's house. He could remember her from childhood already living close, mewed up in mystery, yet capable and authoritarian. He had not understood her then, and could not guess at her now. If she had any secrets, Rayner's father had not told them, and his mother had always been afraid of her.

The door was opened by a nurse, who led him upstairs. He remembered the interior less for itself than as a facsimile of his parents' home. All colour had been strained out of it by sunlight, leaving it husk-dry and mellow with fawns and golds. It resembled a sepia snapshot. The rugs, the curtains, the cane and wicker furniture – all seemed bleached to the same autumnal pallor. Vases of dried flowers and pot-pourri stood in niches like funerary urns, and pervaded the house with a half-dead sweetness. Even the ormolu mirrors appeared to hold in themselves nothing but a clouded, second-hand sunlight. Rayner could not believe that this house could ever be his.

'Aunt Birgit.' He was unsure how to greet her. He could not remember if he had ever kissed those cheeks.

She was sitting on the edge of her chair. Her hand, when he took it, was a sheaf of bones. All the aquiline power of her face had shrivelled to a delicate scaffolding of dis-coloured skin. She said, 'I wouldn't have recognised you.'

He guessed she had cancer. But he realised at once that only her body had withered. Her mind glittered out through two bruised-looking eyes. 'The last years have been hard,' he said.

'Have you eaten? You cannot have eaten. The nurse will get you something in a moment, and then she'll show you to your room. It will be a great scandal in the street that I have taken in a man.' Her laughter was like a cough. Her voice came rasping and thin, transforming the capital's lisp to the sound of a broken wind instrument. And this was how he was to hear it during the next two weeks – so frail, so harmless-sounding: but each word a small incision.

She had arranged everything. Tomorrow in the law courts they would finalise her will: it required only his attendance and a signature. 'If you decide to live in the capital,' she said, 'you may stay here at once. It's as you wish.' It was impossible to tell if she wanted this. In her voice was no hint of either plea or concession: only convenience. He wanted to thank her, but did not know how. It was like thanking someone for his resurrection. But in the end he took her hand and blundered out his gratitude in a con-fusion of thoughts, while she only smiled a little and at last

159

said impatiently, 'Don't thank me. I'm not depriving myself of anything. I will not be here.'

He could not tell, from her shrunk face or voice, what she was feeling. The instruments of expression all seemed broken. He wanted to say: don't you have other legatees? But he might as well have asked: was your life so loveless?

She said, 'Doctor Morena wants to interview you one day next week. He was impressed by your articles on some disgusting skin disease. He'll presumably ask you to join his practice, but I can't imagine you'll want that.'

Rayner frowned in surprise. 'What's wrong with it?'

'Nothing's wrong with it. It's just an ordinary urban practice. But for you I'm sure it would seem unexciting. You've already got a lively partnership in a busy place.'

'Lively, busy . . . yes, it's certainly that!' His aunt, he thought, could have no concept of a place like the town. 'But I don't feel right there.'

Her eyes came swinging over him like pale lamps. All her vitality seemed to have contracted inwards to the sliver of her hawk's nose and the cool gleam of these eyes in their yellowed sockets. In the end, she said, 'Well, once you have the job offer there'll be no problem about the residence permit.'

Rayner wondered again whom she knew, or if the state control had imperceptibly relaxed. Among the mementoes on the tables round them stood photographic portraits of an ex-minister and a marshal. He enjoyed the idea that Aunt Birgit had known secret lovers, but more likely she had been admired for her social distinction and once-formidable intellect. Tentatively he asked, 'Do you have friends in government?'

'A few.' Her lips pursed. 'But they're mostly finished with all that now. And I don't go out any more.' She laughed her dry, coughing laugh. 'You may attend parties in my name. They'll prefer that. You'll meet your old friends.'

'Good.' He longed to meet them now. More than ever, he knew, they would have converged together in their subtle common language, without him. Doubtless they'd laugh at him for becoming provincial. But their old comradeship, he was sure, would override time and difference.

He said, 'You remember my group of friends, don't you? Leon and Adelina?' He watched her face for some reaction, but it stayed inscrutable. 'Gerhard . . . Jarmila?' She only frowned faintly. 'Miriam.'

Then his aunt said starchily, 'Of course I remember them. They were quite a handful.'

'Have you heard anything of them?'

'These days I don't hear about anybody much,' she said. 'But Gerhard's been successful in business, I understand. He went to one of those industrial cities on the coast.' Her eyes clouded in thought. 'But Leon is the waste of a decent boy. I blame his parents. They were openly promiscuous. In fact I remember your father saying, "I won't have my son grow up like that!" Now the boy doesn't do anything. He's been in and out of mental hospitals.' She shook her head. 'But Adelina and Miriam – Miriam Cotta wasn't it? – I haven't heard of them for years. I daresay they married and left.'

As she spoke, pricking him with sadness, Rayner's old group exploded and scattered in his head, then reassembled. He'd imagined them a unity, but of course they were not. Their adult years had splintered them. 'And what about Jarmila?'

'Oh, the little ballerina.' Her voice was touched with intolerance. 'A conceited creature.'

It was then that Rayner remembered. He had felt there was something familiar the moment he entered the hall, and now he realised. It was here, more than twenty years ago, that Jarmila and the others had staged their *Sleeping Beauty* for a group of indulgent adults. He ran laughing out of the room and bounded down the stairs to verify. And momentarily, in his bifocal gaze, the stepped hall became a stage and auditorium, and the cream draperies the back-cloth of a haunted forest. Childishly, he supposed, but it seemed magical at the time, Jarmila and Miriam were tip-toeing back and forth in muslin tutus which shimmered with silver threads.

He panted back up the stairs. 'Do you remember?'

'Of course I remember,' said his aunt. 'That girl played a beauty, while you wound up the gramophone.'

'What happened to her?'

'Jarmila Kullman? She's still living here, but she's never done anything serious. She's quite unsuited to the real world. No, she's never married.'

For some reason this news distressed Rayner even more than that of Leon. Jarmila – beautiful, fine-boned Jarmila – had been the group's mascot. He asked woodenly, 'Do you remember the silver and muslin costumes? I think my mother must have made them.' It was the kind of craft his mother had enjoyed.

'Oh no. They were only paper.'

'*Paper*?'

'Yes,' his aunt said. 'Those were just children's games, you know. Paper and tinsel!'

22

After four days, the city no longer appeared to Rayner in the double-focus of memory. It had become real, and so was subtly deconsecrated. Once or twice he found himself looking back on the town with wonder. It was the town that had become memory now, and from this safe vantage point a thousand kilometres to the north, it seemed to burn in the wilderness with an unholy vigour.

He was still dragging its shadow after him. At the party next door to his aunt, his hostess greeted him, 'So you're the nephew! Let's pray for a miracle in your aunt's health!' But he answered harshly, 'Miracles and liver cancer don't coexist,' and she was visibly shocked.

He felt his own awkwardness. He sipped his schnapps on one side of the room. He had forgotten how people in the city dressed up. The room was a harvest field of coiffured heads, and was filled with their lisping, dreamy accents. People flowed past him like breezes past a crag. They mostly seemed younger than him, but perhaps were not. The women in their low-cut dresses and glacé bows and torques were several of them pretty, and the men full of debonair enthusiasms. He instinctively liked them. But he found nobody to talk with, and did not recognise a soul. They all seemed to partake of the same identity, voluble, optimistic and a little effete.

But after a while people discovered who he was: the nephew who would inherit. They focused him. Two girls came circling round, talking with the vitality of birds. 'Oh, you come from *that* town!' But instead of condescension, he noticed a streak of awe. 'That's where everything's going on now, isn't it?' They seemed to envy him. But their knowledge came from half-read newspapers. 'Don't say the summer's been hotter than here? *Fifty-two* degrees! . . .' They panted humorously. 'Disease? No, we've never heard of any disease. You mean *nobody's* got a cure?' They looked bewildered, 'The desert must be fascinating . . . But *fourteen* murders? So the savages might just walk up and stick an axe in you? We used to have native servants and they were *absolutely* loyal . . .'

Sometimes, imprisoned in his head, he heard Zoë's ribald laughter.

Yet beneath their patter flared an intolerance which appealed to him. Out of their security – the city's isolation and peace – they were furious with injustice, dismayed at inhumanity, sometimes incredulous. He felt as if he'd returned from a battlefront rather than just another town. 'Torture?' demanded one man. 'You mean *our* people do it? They kill them just like that?'

But they seemed to be hung with veils. They could not really comprehend. Away from the hot, fierce streets of the town, from its frightened inhabitants, its searing wilderness, understanding was impossible. Uneasily Rayner felt that compared to these people he was contaminated, and that, by comprehending even a little the paranoia and torture, he came closer to forgiving it. He was even afraid that this might show in his too-easy conversation, in the smoothness with which he sipped his schnapps while talking about death. In a moment, he thought, the indignant man and the two outraged girls – still uncomprehending – might look at him afresh, and turn away.

And from time to time, behind his eyes, Zoë emerged in a soft, disruptive mockery. Once – so vivid was her image – he even thought she said something; but he could not catch her words.

Then he saw Leon. He was leaning against a cabinet with

164

a glass of wine at his lips. He looked unchanged. The slight plumping-out of his face had dispossessed it of any lines.

Leon caught sight of him at the same moment. 'Rayner!'

They embraced, then stared into each other's eyes, reassembling one another. Leon asked, joking, 'Where have you been? Not in that terrible place all this time?'

Rayner was transfixed by Leon's sameness. After his suffering, it was baffling. He raked his hands melodramatically down his own face. 'Yes, fifteen years! And you see what it's done to me!'

Leon gazed at him with something between admiration and recoil. 'I'd have killed myself,' he said. 'I read that the drought had set the savages marauding.'

'They're marauding through people's heads.'

'I heard there'd been fourteen deaths.'

'Yes. I fished two out of the river.'

Leon shielded his eyes. 'How could you stand it?'

'You have to.'

'Well, I suppose you're a doctor, and used to it.' Rayner noticed his lips trembling. His gaze was fixed on the rim of his wine glass. Leon said, 'It's so long ago since you left. How do we catch up?' But perhaps he did not want to, because he went on, 'Those were magic times, weren't they? Do you remember the masked ball at Adelina's? Do you remember . . .?'

Then, unprompted, he launched down a long, mournful river of reminiscence. He recalled picnics, balls and bathing parties, teenage jokes and childish vendettas, abortive loves, clandestine boating expeditions, accidents, all in a tapestry of detail. Rayner could not remember half of them. But to Leon the act of remembering had attained a terrible, all-absorbing meaning. His anecdotes followed one another in a maudlin rush, and the old, fastidious intelligence which Rayner remembered was powerless against it.

At last Rayner intervened, 'You remember twice as much as I do!'

The room had started to empty. The remaining guests stood islanded among the scattered hors d'oeuvres and emptied glasses.

'But it's all somewhere inside you, isn't it? I promise you.' Leon touched his shoulder in confidence, and looked momentarily ashamed as he murmured, 'Have you heard about these psychiatrists? There are lots of them in the city now. Do you know about them? They help you remember your infancy.' He looked bereft. 'It's a kind of healing. Just to remember.'

'Has it been?' Rayner felt a desolate pity for him.

Leon balanced his wine glass on the cabinet. He was a little drunk. 'Not yet.' Then he took Rayner's arm with pathetic urgency. 'You will be staying in the city now, won't you? We've got everything here.' His grip relaxed. 'Too many of the others have gone. Gerhard, Ivar . . .'

'What's happened to Adelina?'

'She married and went away too. She lives in the west somewhere. Very happy.' He picked up his glass again. 'But I see Jarmila sometimes . . . poor Jila . . .'

Then it occurred to Rayner how little he had understood any of their childhoods. They had appeared seamlessly happy and privileged. Yet already serpents were being born. A light tension came fanning up in him when he asked, 'And what about Miriam?'

Leon smiled at him. 'She still lives here. She's had a little girl.'

Rayner felt an obscure, foolish pang. 'I didn't even know she was married.' But what did it matter? After fifteen years she would not be the Miriam he remembered: the girl whose air he'd breathed among the damsel-fish.

Leon said, 'She's not married any more. That didn't last long.'

Rayner knew his heart-skip was as absurd as its hurt had been. But he cried out, 'Tell her to visit me!'

*

Overhung by a tasselled parasol, Aunt Birgit was sitting in the shade. Her eyes were shut. The moving air was laced with the sea, and the box trees in the garden smelt of Italy.

Rayner sometimes sensed that when she closed her eyes like this, sitting straight-backed and perfectly conscious, she was practising death. She never spoke about her illness, but he knew that it was liver cancer from her diet, and from the yellow discoloration in her skin and eyeballs, and that there was nothing to be done. At first he felt guilty that he, a doctor, was living here and unable to save her. Then he realised that his aunt was more reconciled to death than to life. Almost all her relatives and friends had predeceased her, and she would routinely refer to people living not by their Christian names but as 'the Melchert son' or 'the Garcia girl'. The passions and personalities which had shaken her whole generation – and she had been a political liberal during the worst years – had fallen bleakly redundant, together with the fashions and clubs, the film stars and opera singers, even the connotations of certain words, as if meaning itself had preceded her into the dark.

She was not grieving, but stoic and sometimes censorious. She shared with his father, and with himself, a cruel bluntness. He had come to realise that it was pointless to be oblique with her, and now, sitting beside her in the garden, he felt able to say, 'I can't have interested you as a child, Aunt Birgit. Why are you leaving me this house?'

From the parasol's shade she tried to seek him out with her eyes. They flinched against the glare. 'Because I loved my brother, and he always had high hopes for you. You're like him. He cut his own way.' She lifted her hand above her eyes. Their pale glitter reached him at last, but he could not tell what she was seeing. She said, 'You were rather a lonely child.'

Perhaps some loneliness in her, Rayner thought, had gazed out and recognised him. Had she given him the house, then, as an anchor or compensation? But soon

167

afterwards she said, 'You may do what you like with it. It's never been much to me.'

Rayner wondered in astonishment: what, then, was much to her? She had lived here more than forty years.

But she went on stiffly, 'Perhaps this house would remind you too much. No one should live in the past, and yours wasn't easy.'

Rayner said, 'Mother was all right to me. It was only her drinking. You know she couldn't stand it when he died. She lost her grip.'

But his aunt said, 'Whatever she drank for, whether it was loneliness or remorse, drink never cured anything.'

Rayner said edgily, 'Remorse?'

'Well, your father was so much older, and she was a romantic creature.'

Rayner knew, suddenly, that he was above an abyss. Yet his mother's life seemed aeons ago. She stood arranged in his memory, completed by death. She could not now be changed. Whatever was true. On his aunt's lips 'romantic creature' carried no softness. She had always despised his mother. He caught the tremor in his voice: 'You mean Uncle Bernard?'

'That was a foolish young man.' Her lips tightened. 'Your father never liked him.'

'My mother wouldn't have done that.'

'I don't know what he was to her.'

Into the silence Aunt Birgit's cat – a plump Persian – dropped from its tree and settled under her chair. For years Rayner had conceived of his mother only by a handful of mental images, and the last of these – her sallow face, as she climbed into the car which would kill her – flickered up behind his eyes.

He had not been an ideal son. Even before his father's death he had retreated into his own privacy and into the world of his friends. But he wanted to exonerate her, and a hardness appeared in his voice. 'My mother at least gave

168

me my freedom. She never pleaded for my help or made me feel bound to her. I know she was frail, but I loved her. I don't think my childhood was unhappy. Quite the contrary . . .'

His aunt seemed to relent. 'I didn't mean to say she was a bad woman. Only she could be scatterbrained.'

'But she was there when it was important. She even saved my life when I was little. It was only in the last few years she started to break up. My early memories are all of her smiling, laughing . . .'

'When did she save your life?' In his aunt's rasping voice, the idea sounded sentimental.

'During the fire. You remember we had a fire?'

'Yes I do. That was an unfortunate accident. I remember your father had to sack the native maid when he returned.'

'I'd forgotten that.'

'Well, you were only five. We could afford more native servants in those days. They weren't very reliable, and who could blame them? They were paid nothing. This one somehow started a fire which gutted half the house. Luckily she rescued you first.'

'I don't even recall her.' Rayner's memory reached back in ache and puzzlement; it strained at the blue gauzes of smoke, trying to see distinctly. 'I thought it was my mother.'

'Your mother was not in the house.'

'Where was she?'

His aunt looked down and observed her hands. They were glazed with liver spots as big as coins. 'I don't know where she was.'

The nurse emerged onto the terrace, glanced at them, then went back indoors. A pair of hoopoes skittered over the grass. Rayner closed his eyes against the dazzle of the declining sun; its colours swarmed behind his eyelids. He heard children giggling in the garden next door. Aunt Birgit's hand, hanging limp now, discovered the cat under her chair and started weakly to stroke it. For a long time its purring was the only sound in the world.

At last Aunt Birgit said, 'The house, you understand, is only yours if you want it. I wouldn't blame you for not staying in this city. I wouldn't stay if I were a young man.'

Rayner did not know what to answer. But if he lived in the capital, it would not be on this street. He would feel too much a child again. But he said, 'If I decided to sell, it would be nothing to do with the house, only the city.'

His aunt nodded. 'It's always been an awkward site for the capital, you know. It's pretty, but it's not practical.' She eased herself to her feet. 'In the end all our best young minds go to other places. You, for instance, and Gerhard. This is only a place to be a child in.'

He escorted her back to the house. She walked delicately and very upright, as if supported by an unseen stick. Once he took her arm, but she flicked his hand away. He did not know if he revered or resented her.

It was as they were climbing the three steps to the terrace, and he was looking down to where the balustrade met the earth in a rounded finial, that he remembered the lizard. The terrace was identical to the one in his parents' house, and something in the way the stone ball disappeared into the ground, leaving a ruffle of warm dust around its base, awoke in him a memory of the lizard's trial.

Ivar, Gerhard, Leon and he had trapped it while it was basking under the ball. It was a bloated ghekko, the colour of damp earth. Gerhard yelled, 'Let's execute it!' But he might have been teasing Leon, who was squeamish. Their treble voices rose in the dust. 'We'll put it on trial!'

They sat in a row before it. Ivar had secured its leg with a strand of string. It froze, panting. Gerhard picked up a small rock and placed it ceremonially in front of him. 'It deserves to die.'

But Leon had turned white. He was staring at it in fascinated recoil. 'I say we let it go.'

'You would.' Ivar turned to Rayner. Even aged nine, he had somehow seized the initiative and made himself chief judge. 'Gerhard votes for death, Leon votes against. What do you say?'

Rayner demanded, 'What's it done wrong?'

Gerhard thought. 'It eats flies.'

Rayner rebelled. He sometimes hated Gerhard. 'That's just its nature.'

There was silence. Then Ivar nodded, perhaps reluctantly, but repeated, 'That's just its nature. You can't count that.'

'Then you can't count *anything*!' Gerhard said.

'You can,' Rayner answered. 'it's got to be a *nasty* kind of lizard, say, or a nasty bloke — like you!' They scrambled together, fists flailing. Rayner and Gerhard were always fighting.

But Ivar shouted, 'Stop! The trial continues!'

The tousled line of judges reassembled. It was astonishing what power Ivar already had, and an uncanny composure. He seemed to know everything. He appealed to Gerhard, 'What else is wrong with this lizard?'

But Gerhard had no imagination. He glared dourly between Rayner, Leon and the ghekko, and ground his rock impotently into the soil.

At last Ivar said, 'Rayner and Leon vote against, so that's two against one.' He untied the ghekko's leg. Its white cheeks pulsed, but it stayed where it was. 'I declare this lizard okay.'

Leon cried, 'We win!' But he was in the grip of a secret excitement. He couldn't take his eyes from the lizard. Rayner tried to poke it into life, but it remained motionless, like a carving fallen from the balustrade. Only its gills went on pulsing, and once it opened a weak, pink mouth.

At last they grew bored. Gerhard marched home, singing derisively, and Ivar and Rayner scrambled onto the terrace, arguing. Then they sat quiet in the sun, feeling exhausted. Irritably Rayner wondered how Ivar always managed to turn himself into the leader, but he could uncover no method. He doodled with his toes in the dust.

But after a while, just beyond where they sat, they heard a dry, violent pounding. They stared at one another, crept to the balustrade and peered over. Then they saw something which neither of them ever spoke of again: it was too private, too unaccountable. Beneath them, with cold, frenzied blows of the rock, Leon was pulping the lizard to death.

During his last few days, Rayner took to rambling the streets and parks. He was reminded of how beautiful the city was. Unsmirched by industry, the façades of all its public buildings shone in a lustrous stone. They resembled, he thought, a stately theatre set. He peered inside the Opera House, which was showing *L'Africaine*, and watched the guards outside the presidential palace, marching back and forth in their white and gold uniforms. He took coffee under the hanging flower baskets of the shopping arcade. He even spent time identifying the statues in the squares: men in frock coats, mostly, with scrolls and upraised fingers, telling the world things. Sometimes the whole city seemed very innocent.

Occasionally, a little way in front of him, he imagined he recognised the rangy stride of Adelina or the froth of Miriam's curls. But when he drew alongside, the expression which met his would be blank. In fact he saw nobody he knew. And people seemed to move in a languid self-absorption. Their eyes might meet his, but they rarely focused, and he came to associate this dreamy stare with the city: a gaze without penetration, like the becalmed vision of a cat. Whole shops and restaurants and streets were filled with it. It turned them faintly unreal. Even the young women, looking back at him, would only glance away or smile after two or three seconds. A few of them were beautiful. But most looked merely pretty, like mezzo-

172

tints. He could not imagine them losing their tempers or making love. They only made him ache for Zoë: her exuberance and irreverence and unpredictable passions.

Once he saw a cat like hers squeezing through a restaurant doorway and felt suddenly, joltingly sick. He half expected her to follow it out and gather it in her arms.

He wondered where the savages had gone, who years ago had been drafted in as domestic labour, but there was scarcely a sign of them. They had not intermarried, and the few he saw were 'white men's natives', tamed and neat in their suits and frocks. Only once, as if she had stepped out of the wilderness, a wild-looking woman and her young child came striding past him down the central boulevard, inexplicable among the trams and parasols.

Whenever Rayner turned the corner into his parents' street and glimpsed between the ranks of balconies the whitewashed church, he received a momentary sensation that he shouldn't be there, that the whole street belonged to the dead. He had not attended mass for fifteen years, and had lost his faith before that: yet unconsciously he had located belief in this sanctuary near his childhood home, where God perhaps survived inside the comfortable body of the community.

He stepped into the nave. Two or three elderly women were sitting among pews in the pleated chiffon collars which they wore for confession. Nothing had changed. The plaster Virgin still looked at heaven while the tapers died at her feet, and the saints performed their miracles in the stained glass. He went softly into the chancel. He remembered each memorial plaque. Higher up, where as a boy he had offered Anna's crystal to the crucified Christ, the embroidered gold altar cloth was dedicated to the memory of his father.

Then he felt a heart-shaking guilt, as if his apostasy was branded on him. He was standing in a foreign temple. It mattered now that he could not repeat the Creed or drink the wine, and he remembered amazed how for three years he had attended mass in half-belief, or none. Now he was too exacting even to look at the altar's gold Christ. His God had not outlived him in the city, had not been located in space at all, but in time, where He had been lost.

23

Doctor Morena had a creaseless moon-face which looked permanently anointed with skin cream. He apologised for the howl of babies in the surgery – which was mild compared to baby clinic day in Rayner's practice – and settled pleasantly behind his desk. He had known Birgit Sorensen for years, he said – a truly original woman, 'one of the old school' – and had read Rayner's articles on psoriasis with respect. If Rayner should decide to settle in the capital, then ... Conditions, he implied, were more benign than those in the town. Heatstroke and septicaemia were rare, and diseases due to stress were less common than infectious and hereditary ones. But even TB and diphtheria were on the wane; and there were, of course, no industrial accidents, and little alcoholism or venereal disease. The surgical and obstetric wings of the local hospital coped with any problems beyond general expertise.

Smiling back at the beneficent, faintly smug face in the well-appointed clinic, Rayner felt perverse to be hankering after the rumpus of his own. Medically, he knew, it was not the way things should be, but his tough, diversified practice – the chaotic improvising, the follow-up of his patients through the hand-to-mouth hospitals, the hazards of his radiotelegraph service – had become his second nature and stimulus. Out there he was at once more tested, more needed and more self-governing than here. He recognised that he had been tightened to a certain pitch like a violin string, and could not now be undone. A little astonished at himself, he thanked Dr Morena for his offer, but realised

175

that he would decline. He was bewildered at the finality of this, and by his lack of much regret.

But he wanted to go home.

In the sky, as he started back to his aunt, a whispering flock of cranes, heading south, betrayed the deepening autumn. He got off the tram beyond the State Assembly, and entered the skein of familiar streets. His foot was starting to throb, but he was nearly back, and did not care. For the first time, as he rounded the corner into his parents' road, he had the sensation that it existed in its simple essence of iron and stone, and that in the last few hours it had been laid obscurely to rest.

The nurse opened the door to him. She said, 'A Mrs Miriam Eliade called to see you. She said she'd be back in an hour.'

So she was coming. He sat down on a chair in the hall and stared into the mirror opposite. He saw a tanned, shriven face with a fierce chin and sensuous mouth. Already small lines were tearing its forehead and pinching the corners of its eyes. And his hair was receding in two shallow bays. He had hardened, he knew, and perhaps coarsened. Yet he found himself hoping sentimentally that Miriam would be unaltered, that he would be confronted by the vibrant girl he remembered. He went upstairs and changed his shirt. He laughed at himself a little as he combed his hair sideways, like a schoolboy preparing for a date.

When the knocker sounded he sauntered downstairs, restraining his nerves, and opened the door. Then he stood frozen by surprise. He might have opened a door onto the past. It was almost shocking. She stood there in a white dress. The same dark eyes were smiling at him from her brown face. The familiar curls shifted round her shoulders. The same brimming figure radiated health.

For a moment he just stared at her. 'You must be immortal!' Then he burst into laughter and his hands lifted to his own face. 'My God, I look bad.'

176

She kissed him. 'It doesn't matter for men!' But he could feel her gaze raking over him, trying to disinter the nineteen-year-old boy from the thirty-four-year-old man.

His aunt was sleeping, so they sat in the room full of mirrors and faded sun. Her unchangedness mesmerised him. Her skin had kept the glow and clarity of a girl's. The brown vigour of her body seemed to be pouring health into it even as she sat there. From the dive-boat he had carried away an image of this summer skin – a lemony, translucent tissue above pretty blue veins – and had imagined he'd exaggerated it. But here it was, amber against her white dress, a hand's touch from him. He grinned bemusedly at her. Whenever she smiled at him and her eyes crinkled in their short, black lashes, time concertinaed helplessly and they were kissing in the city park again.

But what had happened to her, he demanded, and why hadn't she written?

Well, why hadn't *he* written? He knew she was a hopeless letter-writer. And oh, what had happened to her? *Everything*. She'd got married, had a child, been divorced.

'I was a perfect idiot to marry him! Everybody told me so. But you know me!' Her laughter bubbled up unbidden, and the old vivacity lit her face. 'He was a horse-breeder from the Djaban region. Can you imagine it? *Me* sitting out there! *Ennui*! We had bags of money, of course, but nowhere to go and nothing to do. I don't want to see another horse as long as I live. And I still can't tell a palomino from an Arab. In the end I just couldn't stand it.'

'Didn't that hurt?'

'I didn't let it! Anyway, it was a good experience. I don't think you should regret *any* experience. It's hopeless looking back, isn't it?' She touched her heart. 'I maintain things like that don't just happen. Nothing's wasted! Do you think?'

'God knows why things happen.' In the alcove where they sat facing one another, he could see her head and his

177

multiplied in the mirrors behind each of them, on and on through the distilled sunlight in the tarnished glass. Every time she moved a fraction, the shimmer of her curls thronged into infinity, while his craggy face swarmed in between, until they dwindled and sickened into a greenish distance caused by his aunt's never cleaning her mirrors.

He said, 'What happened then?'

'I came back and lived here,' she said. 'Where else can one go? Now I look after my daughter, who's a monster. Adorable, but a monster. If only she sat still occasionally like my ex-husband, that brute scarcely *moved*! But she takes after me.' Her body wriggled in its low-cut dress.

'What about our old friends?'

'Oh I never really got on with Jarmila, she's too selfish. But I see Leon sometimes.' A small frown crossed her face. 'He's a dear, but *so* introspective . . .' Her eyes glittered at him. 'How strange to see you! All those years ago! Do you remember the picnics above the cliffs? And the diving?'

'Of course I do. Diving was the last time I saw you, when we used each other's regulators.'

'Wasn't it fun?' She shot her ebullient smile. 'Do you remember the reef-shark we saw? And those horrible manta rays. And oh yes, exchanging regulators. Such a peculiar feeling. It was like breathing each other's air, wasn't it?'

'Yes, it was.'

'Once I was doing that with Gerhard and the regulator tore itself out!' One hand fluttered from her mouth. Through the mirrors her fingers multiplied and wavered like seaweed in a drowning green current. 'I haven't gone diving for years. Have you?'

'There's nowhere to dive out there. You're on the edge of desert.' The only deep water was the lake, where Zoë and he had swum and made love.

'Oh yes, I heard about the trouble you've been having. What's been done about the savages now?'

178

'You can't do much. They make their own rules. You just pray for the autumn rains. They've lost a lot of cattle.'

A cloud settled over her determined brightness. He saw, of course, that even she was not quite ageless. When she drew in her chin to laugh, a tiny slackness flickered there, and a ghostly pair of crow's-feet teased her eyes. Yet like the city she remained inexplicably the same. He recalled the pattering and precise rhythm of her talk, and the way laughter suffused it. But she was no longer memory.

She said, 'I don't understand why the savages can't be organised better. It's dreadful just to leave them out there killing farmers. Can't you round them up?'

'If you try to round them up, they evaporate.'

'Well, I don't see why.' She went silent.

He remembered this too: the combative streak which surfaced when there was something she did not understand. He said, 'The savages go their own way. I once took two into my house, so I know.'

'Took two in? Was that any fun?' She was laughing again. She seemed to have upholstered the whole hard world. 'I'd have dreaded coming down in the morning and finding they'd emptied the place!'

She still seemed to find him attractive. Her eyes sparkled over him and she laughed flirtatiously. She must gradually have leaned towards him too, because in the mirrors her teeming heads, raked by a long, dimming cross-fire of sunbeams, had sunk lower than his.

In the end she glanced at her watch and said, 'I have to collect my daughter in a minute. When are we going to meet again?'

'I'm going back tomorrow.'

'You're going back tomorrow! You old killjoy! Oh how sad.' She looked genuinely disappointed, a little. 'I'd see you off if I could.'

Rayner started to laugh with a trace, still, of bitterness. 'I expected that before and you never came!'

She looked at him uncomprehending.

He said, 'Fifteen years ago. When I left.'

She clapped her cheek. 'Yes, oh yes! I remember! I felt awful about that. I really did. It was somebody's twenty-first birthday and I couldn't come. I do remember.' She smiled weakly. 'I do.' Then, 'Why are you laughing?'

She got up to say goodbye. He kissed her hand with a slightly cynical courtliness, which made her slap his head. He had always been a great tease, she said. As she embraced him, he glimpsed in the looking-glass, as if down the avenues of his memory, a hundred Miriams kissing in his arms, until the uttermost rooms held only two insects saying farewell in amber. Then they disengaged, and she said, 'Hope to see you before another fifteen years!'

After she had gone he was chagrined to find tears pricking up behind his eyes. But they were not exactly for her.

In the long-drawn evening, when the sun had dropped behind the terraces but not yet set, Rayner ambled down the unlit street towards the church. He did not go in, but wandered round the outside for a while and laid some flowers by his parents' grave. Then he sat on a bench under the carob trees, while beside him all the wrought-iron verandahs and balconies became baskets of curtained light.

Later he went indoors, expecting to eat supper with his aunt; instead he found that she had weakened and that the nurse had put her to bed. This somctimes happened, the nurse said: the old lady went up and down. But Rayner was leaving early in the morning, and he waited by her bedside. She seemed only intermittently to grasp who he was, addressing him in a different, more familiar tone, as if he were a contemporary, and once she called him by his father's name.

After she had fallen asleep, he went away to pack; but his suitcase was too full to close – he had bought gifts for Zoë,

Leszek and several other friends — and he entered the shower-room to wash off the sweat which filmed him even here. He felt suddenly tired. The water covered his back in tepid bursts. He soaped it idly. Then, as he glanced down at his body, he saw the blemish slapped on it like a leech. It dribbled blackly from one nipple almost to his groin. It had erupted without warning, overnight.

He froze, waiting. Yet he was not struck by disgust, or fear, or even surprise. He touched it tentatively with his fingertips, in recognition. Its chocolate snake gleamed between the runnels of soap. It smeared his ribs like the dirt of reality. It seemed less like a recent eruption than an awesome birth-mark. He let the water trickle over it, skirting sometimes its raised roughness, and remembered it on Zoë's body, and on a hundred others.

24

There was nobody to say goodbye this time, and it was still dark when the train pulled out of the station. But Rayner's carriage was full. He was flanked by a bewildered army conscript and a winder-operator assigned to the mines. Opposite, a young financier and his wife were decrying the airy inexpertise of the capital's bourse, but were nervous of the rumoured cut-throat practices in the town. Beside them sat a gaunt schoolmistress, weeping.

For several minutes, as the capital drifted away from them in a blaze of elusive lights, they all craned from the windows into the soft night, then one by one returned to their seats in silence, while it sank into dark.

Rayner sat through the vacuum of the next hours half asleep and watching the plains ruffle into hills. The carriage air thickened with cigarette smoke and the reek of half-eaten mangoes and salami. He drew down the blinds against the sun. The conscript, who had not travelled before, was sick out of the window, and the desultory talk among the passengers faded out. By late afternoon they had entered the mountains, and the clank of the carriages over bridges and the blurred pulse of their wheels in the tunnels, kept everyone intermittently awake. In four hours they saw no life but wheeling kestrels and a village of native goatherds. It was a land of shale and treeless valleys. Huge boulders had snapped off the mountain tops and rolled down into the streams. Their scree scored the valleysides in unconcluded drifts, and looked still in motion. It was impossible to tell if they had fallen an epoch or a minute before.

After dark Rayner climbed into a top bunk and lay close beneath the static fan-blades. They were black with dead mosquitoes. For the first time he felt the slight, listless fever which his patients had reported. He slid a hand between his shirt buttons and tracked the trickle of disruption over his ribs. But soon afterwards he must have fallen asleep, because an hour later he awoke in pitch dark to a strange stillness and silence. The train had stopped.

He dropped softly to the floor and leant out of the window. Opposite was a wall of mountain, overhung with stars. Hurricane lamps dithered up the track, and faint voices sounded where the engine threw two blobs of light into nothing, and three or four men were trying to pull something from under the cowcatcher.

Rayner remembered that in twenty-four hours he must report for the military expedition. He enjoyed the thought of blamelessly missing it. He could not be court-martialled for a railway accident. Then he fell asleep again, and was woken in harsh daylight from a dream of Zoë by the shudder of the train stirring into life. They were already ten hours behind schedule, and for another five they gasped up the watershed of the massif. They saw no person, no building; only, here and there, the graves of convicts who had died constructing the railway thirty years before.

Then suddenly they were descending, and everybody sensed a change. The air became closer, the sun fiercer. But the blinds flew up and the passengers kept peering out in anticipation until the mountains loosened and began to release them. Then, at last, they glimpsed below, and far beyond, the brilliant, sun-struck wilderness. It spread to a trembling skyline. And Rayner saw, with a surge of relief, that the whole sky above it, from horizon to horizon, was hung with a streaming concourse of clouds.

By the time they had descended to the plain and crossed the empty cattlelands to the suburbs, it was evening. The light and heat had mellowed together. Outside the carriage

183

window the bungalows went by in a mélange of corrugated iron and pink-tiled roofs, among scarlet bursts of flame-trees. The train reached the station and the friendships of the journey ended. The financier was met by a business colleague, the conscript by an army sergeant, the schoolmistress by nobody.

In the familiar streets the shopping crowds jostled with workers going home. Two of Rayner's patients greeted him in passing, and wondered where he'd been. He asked news of the town, but nothing had changed, they said, except the sky. Yet the air was gentler, he felt, and an intangible burden seemed to be lifting. Perhaps the rains would even cleanse away the disease! He started to sing tunelessly to himself. In his absence the landmarks he passed had acquired a little strangeness: the Doric pilasters of the Municipality were sturdier, the mine's flotation mills huger, even the St Vincent de Paul charity shop appeared quainter. At the bottom of his street, the children's roundabout looked more bright and minuscule than before, with its little painted cabins empty.

His own house, when he entered it, might have been abandoned years before. Zoë's rugs and hangings had gone, and the walls rose stark. He found himself staring at things in momentary bewilderment: at the charred circle in the annexe rug, the empty cupboard where her costumes had hung, the stuffed armadillo in its alcove. Everything looked clean and incomplete. Yet only two weeks' mail was in the box, with a notice of confirmation that the army expedition would leave at dawn tomorrow.

He walked back through the rooms, through his own self-inflicted desolation, and once or twice glanced at his face in the mirror as if it must have changed. In one corner of the kitchen he came upon a box which Zoë had packed with five mugs, and left behind. It was as if she had abandoned it there on purpose — like a last, tentative foothold in their union. Tomorrow, or soon after, she would arrive to

184

retrieve it with some blithe allusion to her forgetfulness, and carry it away – if he allowed her – pretending that it had meant nothing.

Then he was engulfed by a confused elation. One by one, he pulled the mugs from their wrappings and hung them back in their places on the dresser. He was glad that she could not see his trembling. Walking through the rooms again, he spread her hangings back on the walls in his imagination, and relaid her rugs over the floors. He pictured her presence there (the house had always been too big for him); he returned her to the sitting-room among her plants, to her dance studio, to the bedroom. In the garden room he even imagined – as naturally as if they were waiting – successors to her lost child.

By now it was dark outside. She must be at the club, he knew, but he gathered up the gifts which he had bought for her and went out into the streets. A light wind was driving new clouds over the stars. Already the pavements had emptied, and the noise of late cars was fading. The distinctive crunch and drag of his own footsteps was the loudest sound he heard. Once a pair of vigilantes crossed the road to stare at him, and a patrol car slowed uncertainly before moving away.

The street where she lived was almost unlit. A single lamp stood like a lighthouse in a sea of dark. He padded across the intervening garden to rap on her flat door. He noticed his hand quivering. But nobody answered, and the windows were curtained. He put his gifts at the base of the doorstep, then did not know what to do. He wanted to wait for her here, to listen for the tap of her approaching feet, and call to her from the trees. But it was two hours before she would return. Her cat appeared in one window and stared at him.

He ripped a piece of paper from his notebook, meaning to post it through her letter-box, then realised he did not know how to write what he wanted to say. He sat down on her doorstep, while the wind sifted through the garden. Tentatively he began: 'These gifts . . .' but stopped, and crumpled up the paper. The returning fever throbbed in his eyeballs. He tore another sheet from the notebook, and inscribed in a hard, clear hand, as if some valve of love in him had opened: *I've come back. Forgive me.*

25

The patrol crossed a treeless savannah where nothing moved. The grass whispered under the wheels, and the cracked earth carried them forward as if over a parquet floor. But they travelled blindly, by compass point, because no landmark – not the faintest ridge or knoll – broke the haze on the horizon.

They had set off in four jeeps and a hush of secrecy before dawn, as if the natives might hear of their departure and somehow send news ahead. This feeling of being observed, which infected all the town, had spread even to the officers – Ivar and a surly lieutenant – who restrained the soldiers from singing or cheering as they left. Their objective, too, was secret.

All morning they rustled across the plain over grasses which thrashed and whined against the truck sides. Then eucalyptus trees and acacia appeared, and airy shrubs which splattered the windscreens with pollen and burnt-out seed-pods. The ground turned noiseless under them. The jeeps spewed up a trail of red dust which penetrated even the men's cartridge-magazines. A few bleached-looking birds twittered in the trees. Although they had long ago left behind any sign of habitation, they twice surprised cattle grazing in the underbush: black or brindled steers which lifted their heads in terror and blundered away through the scrub.

Rayner travelled in the rear jeep, beside the driver. Six soldiers sat facing one another behind, their rifles unloaded between their knees. They had started out exchanging boisterous jokes and lewd songs, but the heat and silence, the lonely immensity of wilderness and – now – their distance from home, had gradually turned them quiet. One by one they had peeled off their battledress shirts and sat sweating bare-chested, but the faces under their bush hats had gone uneasy. Rayner could feel the perspiration dropping down his ribs under his army shirt, but dared not take it off. He asked the driver, 'Where d'you think we're headed?'

'Dunno, sir. Reckon it's due south. But there's nothing there.'

Already Rayner was nervous of their objective. He guessed they were making for a place where the savages presented a solid target. It would be typical of Ivar to mete out punishment as if the natives were a coherent nation, and a few raiders in one part of the wilderness identical to an isolated clan in another. The last clash had occurred fourteen years ago, Rayner remembered, against a savage raiding party sixty strong. No white man had been killed because the natives had never reached spear-throwing distance. The soldiers had simply gunned them down at a range of 120 metres and left their corpses to the sun.

He asked the driver, 'Were you told to expect anything in particular?'

'No.' The man was squinting into dust. 'Just maybe a battle.'

Now the forest had resolved into a harsh simplicity of red earth and white trees. It looked as if the rains of some earlier year had melted the ground into a rosy sea and smeared it over the jungle for hundreds of kilometres, until it had solidified again into this coral-coloured pavement. The gum trees shone matt-white, like plaster-of-Paris, but often their bark had peeled back to reveal black, coagulated innards, as if the trees had burnt to death from inside.

They stopped three times to eat or rest. The soldiers debouched from their jeeps and dispersed among the trees to smoke against orders, or defecate. They were a motley lot, Rayner thought, many of them young and jittery. With each stop they seemed to trust the forest less, until at evening they reclined with their backs to the trucks and their rifles at their sides.

'You go into that fucking scrub,' said the platoon sergeant, 'and in ten minutes you'll be history. He'll come and stick a spear in you and you won't even see him.'

Once the convoy slid to an unplanned halt. Rayner saw nothing at first but a screen of trees, then the soldiers clambered out. He found them in a wan semi-circle, their rifles drooped. In front of them, sunk to its axles in the scarlet earth, was a burnt-out jeep. Grey termite hills rose round it like tombstones. It must have lain rotting here for fourteen years, ever since the last troubles. But nobody, not even the sergeant or the half-caste corporal, could recall the incident in which it had been lost. It simply rested there inexplicably, pillaged of any identification. For a moment they gazed at it in silence, while butterflies flickered through its empty windscreen. Then Ivar ordered them to move on.

Rayner's driver just murmured, 'Christ!'

For a long time now the convoy had travelled over an earth prickling with termite hills. There were millions of them. They covered the ground like a fakir's bed, and seemed to go on for ever. The lighter ones crumbled in powdery bursts against the jeeps' bumpers, but the drivers wove between the larger ones in a wearying eternity of curves. So dust thickened and stifled the sky worse than before. The whole earth, Rayner felt, must have been sifted through the intestines of these termites. It caked the men's bodies like a darkening skin.

Yet to Rayner, dreaming of Zoë, the forest had become attractive, and oddly restful. And its lifelessness, of course, was an illusion. The trees flashed with phosphorescent green and red parrots, and along the way a flock of blood-breasted cockatoos rose screaming from under their wheels. He even had the idea that he might find the old savage and

189

his daughter wandering here, although he knew they could not have come so far and that they had taken another direction.

Towards sunset the convoy crossed a region charred by bush fires. Eucalyptus trees still writhed from the ground, or had fallen all of a piece in white trunks whose pith had festered through them like rust breaking through paint.

At dusk, beyond this double desolation, Ivar called a halt. There was no knoll or water-hole to shelter by, not even a thicker growth of trees. They simply stopped. Some of the soldiers pegged out tents, but nobody used them. Instead they manoeuvred the jeeps into a vestigial square, and rolled out their sleeping-bags in the dust. When they unloaded their stores from the converted gun carriage limber, they found that the dust had penetrated even here, insinuating its grit into the bread and pressed beef, into everything except the water.

The men sat in broken circles by their hurricane lamps. On all sides the shrill of the cicadas rose in a deafening curtain, drowning even the clink of the mess tins and the desultory conversation. The troopers smoked nervously in the gathering dark. They talked in mutters, as if the forest was listening, and those who had fallen asleep lay with their rifles at their sides.

'How was the capital?'

Rayner looked up to see Ivar, bare-chested. He held a lantern in one hand and a cartridge belt in the other.

'Much the same.'

He was surprised when Ivar sat beside him and stood his lantern between his feet. Perhaps Ivar had forgiven him, he thought, rather as he would pardon a wayward child, and Rayner even felt a foolish redemption. How typical of Ivar to elicit this pang of gratitude for his friendship! And after a while it seemed natural that they should be sitting here together – two old friends – rather than with Ivar's grim lieutenant, and nothing seemed to have changed. With Ivar he had the illusion that nothing ever changed.

'So you didn't think of staying in the capital?'

'No,' Rayner said warily. 'I've got too used to the town.' In the lamplight Ivar's expression remained obscure, but in case it flickered with 'I told you so', Rayner added, 'All the same, it's a beautiful city. It's clean. It's quiet. There's a harmoniousness that you miss in the town.' He wondered if Ivar understood what he was talking abut. 'You can smell the sea.'

Ivar said, 'All the same.'

'Yes,' Rayner said. 'All the same.' He laughed.

Out of the forest the scream of the cicadas hid the silence. A light wind was sieving through the trees, and he noticed that half the stars were lost in cloud. It was hard to believe that the wilderness and the capital coexisted in one country.

'Did you see any of our gang?' Ivar asked. 'Or have they all gone?'

'Some have gone, some have stayed. Gerhard left ages ago . . .'

'I know. We've kept in touch.'

'But Leon and Jarmila are still there, although I didn't see her.' He realised that he had purposely avoided Jarmila, who had once symbolised them all. 'But Leon was a mess. He'd been in mental hospital.'

'He was always pathetic.'

'But he was sensitive and interesting. I don't know what went wrong.' But whatever it was, Rayner thought, had gone wrong from the start. He remembered the lizard. 'And I saw Miriam.'

'Ah, Miriam.' She was the kind of girl Ivar called 'a handful'. He and she had never much liked one another. He said, 'She was tough.'

'Tough?' Rayner let this fly away unchallenged, like something passing in the dark he could not grasp.

Around them the soldiers were starting to extinguish

their lamps. Some of them had pulled the linen envelopes from their sleeping-bags as protection against the mosquitoes, and were stretched out beneath them. The night had cooled a little. Ivar continued to sit bare-chested, slapping the gnats as they landed on him, while Rayner sweated secretly under his shirt, and sensed himself advancing to a confrontation. One of the conscripts whimpered in his sleep, then went quiet. Over the soft earth of the camp's perimeter the boots of the duty officer made the faintest, warning crunch as he moved from sentry to sentry. Soon theirs was the only lamp left shining. Now its light picked out all the rounded contours of Ivar's face, everything so smooth and gradual in it, folding one feature into the next. Rayner looked at him.

'Where are we going?'

Ivar's tone never changed. 'South-south-east.'

Years and years of schoolboy power-play grated on Rayner as he said, 'I think I know. There's only one place on the map out here. A native holy place. You told me yourself.'

Ivar said almost courteously, 'It may be holy to them. They've got some war idol there.'

'That was missionary talk.'

'The missionaries were the only ones who'd been there.'

'Plenty of natives go there,' Rayner said. 'One old fellow even told me about it, said it was a place that used to connect their heaven with earth. He spoke of it as a kind of mourning site.'

'That may be, but I never heard of it. Missionary reports tend to be reliable.' Ivar's words fell so balanced, so reasonable, Rayner thought, they turned other people's insane. And Ivar still had to retain the power of inflicting uncertainty when he added, 'But I did not say that place was our objective.'

Rayner felt the return of his fever in a faint, damp caress across his forehead. It seemed purposely to be reminding him of itself. He said, 'Out here the native clans are all different from the ones near town. The old man told me some of the names, but I've forgotten them.' He had a fancy that the forest would echo them back. 'Anyway, they're different.'

Ivar said, 'But they're still savages.'

He had replaced his bush cap as if intentionally to shadow his face. But his body expressed him just as eloquently: a plastic trunk whose limbs showed little hair and no obvious muscle. All its parts flowed together, as if melded by subcutaneous fat, and made his movements boneless as a snake's. Rayner imagined Zoë in his arms, and felt momentarily, wretchedly, estranged from her. His voice came angry:

'So you think you've a right to kill any native you find? Are you planning to wipe out a few then, as a sop to the town? Get yourself promoted? Why don't you drive back and get the bastards who murdered those farmers, instead of looking for a soft target?'

Ivar said implacably, 'You know very well that this is the only target. The others fade away.'

'It's an irrelevant one,' Rayner said. 'People just come there on pilgrimage. How will you know they've had anything to do with the town?'

'We'll know if they're bellicose.'

'Of course they'll be bellicose! With thirty armed men arriving!'

'That will be up to them.'

With Rayner it was an obscure item of belief that a man who planned to kill innocents must in some way be ill, perverted. But Ivar's voice continued almost gently impersonal, and when Rayner hunted back into their boyhood he could remember no time when Ivar had been cruel. But he heard himself say, 'You're not the same fellow I used to know, Ivar. I used to think you were, but you're not.' Then he recalled the moment on his aunt's terrace a few days before. 'Do you remember when we caught that lizard? It was you who let it go.'

Ivar said impatiently, 'Don't get sentimental with me. These people are as savage as their name.' He was nearly angry at last. 'They've murdered fourteen of our own people. If that lizard had attacked me, I'd have stamped on it.' He leant down and extinguished the lantern at his feet as if to end this talk. 'And I'll stamp on these people too.'

Now that the lamp had died, they could see more clearly the sleepers in the camp. The starlight barely touched them, but in their white envelopes they lay row by row, like victims in a morgue. Then Ivar murmured, 'Odd of Leon . . .'

'Yes.' Occasionally Rayner felt as if Ivar's only decency lay in the past, in the capital, in his remembrance. But he didn't say anything more.

Then Ivar got to his feet, strapped on his revolver and walked away without a word to check the sentries, while Rayner at last threw off his shirt and sprawled out on his sleeping-bag. In the dark his betraying rash might have been any other shadow. He felt the sweat dry over his chest. When he shut his eyes his mind dazed under the dinning of the cicadas, which sometimes splattered down on his naked body. But he did not sleep. Somehow Ivar's childhood knowledge of him, and his of Ivar, made their antagonism more painful, as if they had judged each other's deepest self, and found it valueless.

He turned on his stomach and folded the sleeping-bag over him. His eyes closed against its roughness. Then, mentally, in mixed bitterness and passion, he lifted Zoë out of Ivar's arms and returned her to his own.

For an hour after dawn they travelled in coolness. The ground was shadowed and the sky still pale, with a few clouds, and the grass formed an amber ground mist under

194

the trees. The land seemed to be sighing under them. It lifted to unnoticeable ridges from which they glimpsed low ranges swimming in haze along the horizon. For a while a dried river bed carried them between its banks, then out again into a silvery wash of porcupine grass. Once or twice isolated hillocks appeared, their rocks like cinders heaped together, stuck with a few acacias. Twice the officers mounted these with binoculars and compass, but Rayner could not be sure what preoccupied them. Sometimes they seemed to be reassessing their line of approach, but often they stared at the sky where for the first time among the light clouds a few floated dark-edged, as if some artist had failed to integrate them. So the rain, ironically, had become a threat. The first downpour, he knew, would glaze the whole land in water within a few hours, mulching the earth to a slippery pink mud where even the jeeps would gain no purchase.

But by mid-afternoon the clouds were still high and few. For hours the hills had retreated before the convoy in dim palisades, but now one group separated itself from the rest. It was barely two hundred metres high, but in this flat land it rose harsh and precipitous, topped by porous crags like a man-made wall. At its foot, where it broke into gorges, the jeeps could go no further, and the men disembarked into a soft, still air. It was utterly silent. The scarps fell to their feet in a debris of shale. On the summits the north-west wind had twisted all the trees one way, but in this stillness you could believe that no breeze had ever disturbed the place.

They entered the bluffs in single file, with two Lewis gun sections bringing up the rear. The way was no more than a shallow defile. Their boots clanged on its rocks. Once it opened into a stony valley and the first signs of human life appeared: a small saltpan where skins had been staked out to cure. Until now Rayner had hoped vainly that the place was uninhabited, but soon afterwards they passed a quarry littered with silcrete flints, and a pair of graves.

He edged up the line of march until he was trudging behind the half-caste corporal, and asked him, 'Who are the people here?'

The man turned a blank face on him. 'They used to be Yiljerong.' He turned his back again. 'But I heard people come here from everywhere now.'

'They're not hostile?'

'I don't know what they are. They're not my people.'

Next moment, with bewildering suddenness, the rocky slopes dropped behind them and they were advancing under trees. With every step these thickened inexplicably round them, until they were moving down a dense, sunless glade. Giant silkwoods lifted from the shadows thirty metres or more, and tossed down a tangle of lianas or spun them overhead from branch to branch. Enormous they seemed, festooned with their creepers and lichen, and after the open savannah the damp smell of the rotted trunks and dark earth rose to the men's nostrils with a fetid closeness. They went nervously now. Nobody spoke. The rifles slipped from their shoulders and into their arms. And their range of vision had dwindled drastically. Among the thronging trees a host of savages might have touched them with their hands. Rayner, moving in the centre of the column, could not glimpse Ivar, near its head. Momentarily he forgot what the soldiers might do, and felt the threat of a spear tip in his back.

Then they came upon the explanation for this fertility: a deep, auburn river. It had risen somewhere higher in the bluffs, and must escape by another gorge to die far out in the wilderness. But for the moment it carried its rain forest luxuriantly between the cliffs. Turtles and thin black fish were swimming under the bank, and big trees had slumbered into the water, which was already brown with the tannin of rotted vegetation.

As the column advanced, it was clear to Rayner that the savages must know they were coming. The natives' traces were all about. A maze of stone fish traps ruffled the shallows, and he noticed a midden of shells in a water-hole near the shore, where mussels had been baked in the earth and eaten. He remembered the mussel-shell necklace which the old man had given him, and was touched again by a fear that the couple might have reached here.

But there was still no sign of anybody. Even the mosquitoes seemed to have gone. The soldiers tried to tread lightly, but the forest floor was a matted commotion of fibres and palm branches, friable as bones underfoot. Their march across it detonated like pistol shots.

Only once, the column stopped to listen, and the forest fell silent. A diluted light survived here, like sunlight infiltrating a crypt. Parrots flew through its half-darkness. But all Rayner could hear was the rasp and click of leaves falling through branches to the ground. He prayed that the savages had taken fright and might simply watch from hiding places until the troops had gone; he even imagined a reception party at the end of the path, stately and bemused, with a basket of doughy welcome-cakes.

But instead the track ended in an empty space and a rearing cliff. The dying sunlight streamed in their faces. The scarp might have been no more than fifty metres high, but loomed immense in its suddenness: a red-rocked peninsula swept on its far sides by the river. Its size and clarity, cut by the brown water, proclaimed: this is a holy place.

The column shambled to a halt on the edge of the clearing, which was ringed by stones as if for ceremony, and Rayner saw that in its centre stood a limestone pinnacle. The soldiers sat down in an exhaustion of heat and nerves, while Ivar and the lieutenant consulted quietly. Rayner took the half-caste corporal by the arm and turned him towards the pinnacle. 'What is that?'

The man gazed at it with the faint knot of savage puzzlement, and said, 'It's something they worship.'

He seemed reluctant to walk over to it, but Rayner led

him. A polished monolith six metres high, it grew more awesome as they reached it. It sprang from the flat earth with the lone momentum of a tree, and its base was piled with baskets of roots and berries.

Rayner said, 'It's not a god.'

'No. These people don't make their gods.' The corporal apparently wanted to dispel his mistakes, but not to supply answers. Perhaps he did not have any. But he said, 'This stone is more like a memory.'

'A memory of what?'

But the man pursed his lips and gazed up at the cliff. It was impossible to tell if he was being protective of native sanctities, or was just sensitive about his own mixed blood. Then Rayner added, 'Is it the tree?'

The corporal turned his back and scrutinised the offerings. 'Yes, they have some myth that this stone led up to heaven. Like a tree. You could climb up and down it.' He touched it with one hand, tentatively. 'Who told you about that?'

'An old fellow I once treated. He said the tree was felled. And that was when everything began to go wrong.'

The sergeant's boots scraped behind them, and the corporal's voice, which had been wary and a little sombre until then, changed. 'That's right, ever since then these poor fuckers have been lost,' he said. 'They want to climb back but they can't. So they're stuck down here like the rest of us.'

Rayner recalled the old man's sketch of the tree in the dust; he remembered his own childish illusion that perhaps the savages' stillness meant beatitude; and he felt a remote sadness for them all. Then the corporal straightened from examining the offerings with a sharp '*Eh*!'

'What is it?'

Beneath the panniers of food he had uncovered coconut bottles in bark containers. They gleamed dark, like hand grenades. 'Water . . .' He murmured more to himself than to Rayner or the sergeant. '*Djannu.*'

'What's *djannu*?'

The corporal glanced at the sky but did not answer.

The sergeant demanded: 'What the hell's *Jah-noo*?'

Rayner added quietly, 'Do they try to water the tree?'

'Yes.' The corporal shrugged almost angrily. '*Djannu* is a kind of ceremony. My father . . .' But he stopped and added expressionlessly, 'They try to stop the sun going down.'

The sergeant said, 'They *what*?'

The corporal stared back at him. At that moment, it was impossible to tell if he was a soldier or a native. He said, 'They try to turn back the sun.'

'For Chrissake!' The sergeant's laughter bellowed in the silence as he lumbered back to his men.

Rayner asked quickly, gently, afraid that the corporal would also go away, 'Do they believe they can do that?'

The man said, 'Yes, they believe one day it will work. That if they stop the sun dying everything will be all right again.' Then he himself laughed, but like a thin echo of the sergeant's. 'People will believe anything, eh!'

The men were reassembling. The officers, Rayner noticed, had opened the flaps of their holsters, and the Lewis-gunners carried their firearm at the hip. As he fell in line, he guessed they were planning to ascend the bluff.

For several minutes they wound directly below it, and were fearfully exposed. Rayner saw every man's face clenched as he glanced up. The skyline of the cliff became terrible. Their rifles swivelled and jerked in their hands. At any moment the sky above them might erupt with men and the air whisper down a rain of spears.

Another path led them up. Under their boots the toeholds in the stone came worn and small, gouged by bare feet. Hoarse bird cries shrilled in the chasm. Every time Rayner turned, his first-aid box banged against the stones and the men had to sling their rifles over their backs to claw themselves higher. He had the sensation that they were being beckoned up. The way could have been held by a single native tossing rocks. Yet nobody appeared.

Then the path levelled out and below them they saw the whole oasis from which they had come, locked in its gorge by the infant river. Beyond it, the sky of the wilderness was thickening and dimming into violet light as the sun declined, and a pair of eagle hawks circled over nothing.

By now the soldiers had clambered to the summit and were reforming. In front of them, as they followed the cliff's rim, the plateau at first looked empty. Then, where a long promontory reached into space, they saw that the rocks were alive with men. The savages had not yet emerged fully onto the spur, and only their heads were visible among the shrubs, but they seemed to number hundreds and even from this distance Rayner saw that their faces were painted a dead, unnerving white.

Ivar yelled an order and the patrol took cover. The troopers crawled into line and steadied their rifles on the boulders. Even the Lewis-gunners folded their bipods and wedged their barrels between rocks. But in front of them all, where the plateau's curve separated them from the promontory, gaped sixty metres of empty air. Rayner lay on his stomach a short way from Ivar, and stared across.

At first, nothing happened. The distant outcrops and acacia bushes only stirred slightly with a half submerged life. Then, in twos and threes, the savages started to materialise and coalesce. Their naked bodies were whitcned by ritual designs, which appeared to clothe them, and they were clasping shields and swinging thongs. They were still emanating from the rocks when the vanguard broke into a lope – more than two hundred men, they seemed – merged in a long phalanx which rolled and undulated along the plateau's brink. The soldiers' barrels were already following them when Ivar yelled out 'Prepare to fire!'

Rayner turned his head in horror. The order had sounded jubilant, but he could see no expression under Ivar's cap.

200

And now the barrels were levelling on either side of him. The Lewis-gunner at his elbow advanced the snout of his gun beyond the rocks and tensed the butt against his cheek. Ivar was crouched on his haunches, staring through binoculars. They all went still.

Yet the savages were not advancing towards them along the plateau's edge, but filtering onto the spur above the chasm. Their lope was less a run than a light, ritual stamping, which scarcely carried them forward. They were not facing the soldiers at all. By now the last of them had issued from the rocks, and the whole procession began to ripple and dance along the promontory. They were barely eighty metres away, and within helpless range. But they moved forward oblivious, with a plunging, tremulous motion towards the spur's end.

Ivar bellowed again, 'Prepare to fire!' Rayner twisted round and their eyes met. Ivar was pouring sweat, and his lips tensed back from his teeth. He jerked his eyes back to his binoculars.

It was impossible that the savages had not noticed the patrol. It was lit up on its cliff top like a stage set. But above the slow-motion pitch and throb of the natives' legs and torsos, all their heads were staring in front of them beyond the headland's drop to where a crimson sun was falling towards the earth. They seemed to be moving on a different stratum of time. With their hair and beards hardened by pipe-clay into clinking locks, and their bodies quartered with bars and diagonals of chalk, they looked coeval with the rocks on which they trod. And when Rayner glanced behind him he was astonished to see a crowd of women and children gathered within a stone's throw – women in bark and sedge cloaks, tattered dresses, kepis – all gazing at the spectacle over the soldiers' heads.

He sank his face onto the boulder in front of him and shut his eyes. He waited for the final order. The lints and bandages in his kit would not suffice for a tenth of the wounded. But instead of gunfire there rose from across the gulley's silence a rhythmic, high-pitched singing. It wavered over to them with an uncanny melancholy, and when Rayner looked up again he saw that the savages had reached almost to the end of the spur, and that their heads were thrown back. In front of them, and level with their bodies, the sun was descending and the whole horizon reddening. He realised that a different order had been passed down the line. The level gleam of rifles had gone. Their barrels now rested upright against the rocks, or on the ground. The Lewis-gunner had plucked the cartridge belt from its breech, and Ivar was leaning forward against a boulder with his head turned away.

Rayner stared back across the chasm, with sweat dripping into his eyes. He could make out the painted countenances on the natives' shields now and the jostling, whitened faces above them, and the feathered tassels on the ceremonial thongs. As he watched, the natives' dancing trembled to a halt at the edge of the drop. Nothing intervened now between them and the sun. Their keening rose to a heart-breaking crescendo, and some of them lifted long, cylindrical wooden horns to their mouths, like monstrous bassoons, which blared and moaned under the chanting.

All around Rayner the soldiers were standing up in full view and gazing across the chasm, uncomprehending. Their rifles strewed the rocks. The sun burnished the earth round them and lit their astonished faces. Some of them sat speechless on the boulders. The sergeant, who had just noticed the women crowded along the ridge behind, kept muttering, 'What's happening here? What the hell's happening?'

By now, at the headland's end, the savages were massed in a coppery glow of bodies, their shields fallen to their sides. As the sun touched the skyline, the singing and the bray of the horns quickened with pathetic urgency. Rayner felt a foolish grief for them. Their sounds intertwined in a

202

wavering threnody, which echoed less like the prayer of humans than the mourning of some unearthly animal. Perhaps it was a distortion of the atmosphere which delayed the sun on the wilderness's rim. But for an instant – so Rayner thought – its red circle and the sharp-edged clouds froze in the sky.

Then, inexorably, yet half against his expectation, the sun was halved, then quartered, by the black edge of the wilderness, and disappeared.

At first, while scarlet clouds littered the sky, all the force of the chanting continued. Then, in slow groups of two or three, the natives began to disperse back over the promontory, and the sounds broke up and faded away. Momentarily, from the point where the sun had vanished, there radiated upwards an enigmatic flush, as if a furnace had been lit just beneath the horizon. Then this too retreated, and left only a pallor over the desert.

For a day and a night the convoy made its way back over the bush. Even a distant fall of rain might have stranded them beyond some swollen river, and the officers ceaselessly scanned the sky while the dark-bottomed clouds put on weight and multiplied.

A mechanical failure delayed their progress for four hours, and one of the water-drums sprang a leak and emptied away unnoticed. But mainly the going was easy. The soldiers bellowed jokes from one vehicle to another, and at night the lurch and jolt of the jeeps seemed barely to disturb their exhausted bodies. One man became feverish, and Rayner could only treat him with cold compresses on a truck floor, and drug him. But by dawn of the second day they were crossing the familiar savannah – now piebald with cloud shadows – and were less than two hours from the town.

As they passed between derelict farmhouses, where a few cattle still stood, the first drop of water hit the windscreen, and Rayner, looking up at a sky which had been void for half a year, saw the massed rain clouds unfurl over the earth.